BAILEIGH HIGGINS

Primordial Earth - Book 9

The Extinction Series - A Prehistoric, Post-Apocalyptic, Sci-Fi Thriller

First edition

This book was professionally typeset on Reedsy.
Find out more at reedsy.com

Contents

Acknowledgments

Thank you to Christian Bentulan for the stunning book cover design. You can check out his portfolio at http://www.covers bychristian.com. He's an amazing artist.

Plus, a huge shoutout to everyone else for their support and help, and to all the fans and readers out there. I truly appreciate you all!

Dedication

This book is dedicated to all my friends and family. It hasn't always been an easy road, but I am here because of all of you. Thank you, and may we have many more tomorrows together.

Prologue - Lt. Cummings

Lieutenant Cummings eyed the gates of Vancouver with guarded excitement as they approached. It had taken them three days of nonstop travel to make the trip from Prime City, and he was glad to be home. His wife, Marie, would be ecstatic if she knew he was back. However, he wanted it to be a surprise and didn't radio ahead to send her a message. *I'll see you soon, darling.*

The Humvee, driven by Sergeant Horton, stopped at the checkpoint. The other two Humvees followed suit, and silence fell while they waited for instructions from the guards. A tall man wearing a thick coat sauntered over, protection against the chill of winter.

He tipped his hat at Lieutenant Cummings. "Good day, Sir. Please, state your business."

"Lt. Cummings reporting for duty," Tomi replied with a terse nod. He flashed his ID card, and the guard jumped to attention.

"Welcome back, Lieutenant Cummings," the guard said, waving at the gate. "Open up and make it quick!"

The gate opened with a ponderous groan, and two more guards jogged over, guns at the ready. They gave the all-clear after a brief inspection, and Tomi was allowed inside the city with his crew.

"Thanks," he said, nodding at the guards before turning his attention to his surroundings.

After being gone for almost three weeks, he appreciated Vancouver with its advanced technology and living conditions even more than before. Especially after seeing Prime; a dynamic city but one teetering on the brink of ruin.

He missed the fresh greenery of summer, however. With the cold season in full swing, the trees were bare, and the grass brittle and brown. It gave the place a dismal feel, and he could well understand those who succumbed to seasonal depression. Even so, he couldn't wait to see his wife again and longed to sleep in his own bed. For that, he could handle the lack of sunshine and cheer.

"It's good to be home," Private Linda Longo said, echoing his thoughts.

"Yup. I can't wait to see Charlotte," Sergeant James Horton added.

"Who's Charlotte?" Linda asked. "A girlfriend?"

Private Sonja Barnes snorted. "It's his cat."

"A cat?" Tomi asked.

"You named your cat Charlotte?" Linda added.

"Why not?" James replied. "She's part of the family."

"More like your only family," Linda said with a chuckle.

"Don't be mean," James said. "Who's waiting for you at home?"

"I'm married," Linda said with a smug smile.

"So am I," Sonja said.

"Lieutenant, back me up here," James pleaded, flashing him a desperate look.

"Sorry, Sergeant. Can't help you there," Tomi replied, flashing his wedding ring.

"Well, Charlotte's all the family I need," James said, grumbling beneath his breath. "At least she doesn't get mad when I'm gone for too long."

"Touché," Linda said.

"I'll give you that much," Sonja added with a laugh. "My hubby gets quite huffy when I go on long trips."

"See what I mean?" James said. "Charlotte's not like that. She understands."

"Weirdo," Linda said.

Tomi shook his head and gazed out the window. He was tired and longed for a hot bath and a solid meal. Something that didn't come out of a tube or a packet. A beer would be even better. Ice cold with the condensation dripping off the sides. The vivid image made his mouth water, and he turned to James. "Step on it, Sergeant. There's a beer with my name on it waiting for me at home."

"Now you're talking!" James crowed, jamming his foot on the gas.

They sped up, followed by the other two Humvees, and within minutes they reached their destination: A walled parking lot that belonged to the government. They waited for the security guard to take their details at the entrance. Afterward, he let them through, and they made straight for the warehouse at the far end.

They checked in their guns and equipment, keeping only their personal belongings aside. Once they were finished, Lieutenant Cummings assembled the crew from all three vehicles. "I'm not one for speeches, and I know you're all anxious to get home, so I'll keep it brief."

Expectant faces gazed at him: Horton, Barnes, Longo, and the rest. All solid, dependable, Grade A fighters. Even

Thompson, the worst cook in the entire universe, and Plumm, who packed a few extra pounds. Probably because he was the best cook in the whole universe. *A solid crew.*

"Thank you for having my back on this mission, guys. I couldn't have asked for a better team. Not now. Not ever," Tomi said. "Now get out of my sight. I'm sick of the lot of you."

Cheers rose in the air, and the group said their goodbyes. Within seconds they dispersed, each making their way home. Cummings lingered, finalizing the paperwork and signing off on the weapons, ammunition, vehicles, equipment, and supplies.

Afterward, he made his way to the Mayor's office to debrief. He hoped it would go fast, handled by an overworked aide who didn't give a rat's ass about his mission. He could ramble off a quick report, backed by a written statement on the morrow, and go home. The sooner, the better.

When he was shown to the Mayor's office instead, he knew he was shit out of luck. Resisting the urge to run, he resigned himself to a long, tedious session.

Maeve Finley stood behind her desk, the epitome of polished grace accompanied by a practiced smile and smooth manner. Her gray suit was immaculate, her nails manicured, and her hair smoothed into a french bun—the perfect politician.

She turned toward him when he entered and extended her hand. "Lieutenant Cummings. I trust your mission met with success?"

"It did, Madam Mayor," he answered, reluctantly shaking her hand. Her skin felt cold to the touch, like marble.

"Please, sit down," she said, waving at a chair.

He hesitated for a brief moment, wishing there was a way out, but there wasn't. He was trapped. With an inward sigh, he took the proffered seat and sat down.

"Tea? Coffee? Water?" Maeve asked. "You must be worn out after such a long trip."

"No, thank you, Madam Mayor," Tomi said.

"Something stronger, perhaps?" Maeve said, walking toward a side table topped with a silver tray, a brandy decanter, a bucket of ice, and crystal glasses.

Tomi shook his head, but she ignored him and poured two glasses. The amber liquid glowed in the light, and he swallowed hard.

"Do you take ice with your drink? I do. I find that it makes for a crisper finish," she said, adding a few blocks to each glass.

She walked toward him and held out the brandy. Unable to refuse, he accepted. "Thank you, Madam Mayor."

She returned to her desk and sat down. Raising the glass, she said, "Cheers to another successful mission, Lieutenant Cummings."

Tomi returned the gesture and took a sip. The brandy was smooth and full-bodied. It went down like silk, and he arched his brows in surprise. "I didn't think stuff like this was still available after the Shift."

"Really? I'll have my aide deliver a bottle to your home tomorrow. Consider it a gift for your efforts," Maeve said.

Tomi stared at her, taken aback. In all his years in Maeve Finley's service, she'd never given him a gift. *She wants something, but what?* "Thank you, Madam Mayor."

"Oh, it's nothing," she said, waving it off with one slender hand. Taking another sip from her glass, she leaned forward in her chair. "Now, tell me about the mission and leave nothing out. I want to know everything, especially about Prime City and its people."

"Yes, Madam Mayor," Lieutenant Cummings said, clearing his throat. He filled her in on all the details in terse tones, leaving nothing out. He also told her what he'd observed in Prime during his stay.

Afterward, she leaned back in her chair and nodded. "Interesting."

Tomi inclined his head but remained silent. He had no idea what she wanted from him and knew he had to wait until she showed her hand. *I just wish she'd get a move on. I don't have all day.*

After a few seconds, she asked. "In your opinion, would an alliance with Prime and its people be of benefit to us?"

"Yes," Tomi answered without hesitation.

"Why?"

"Because they are desperate. They need outside help, and they know it. They are hungry for growth and expansion and will do anything to get it."

"I see. In that case, I will authorize the release of a third shipment containing food, medicine, clothes, and basic supplies."

"That will help, especially during the winter," Tomi conceded, still wondering what any of that had to do with him.

"If they are agreeable to trade with our city, I will send another shipment with seeds, raw materials, and experts to help advance their way of life. In time, they could have a steady supply of electricity, clean water, food, proper medical care, and schooling for their children. If they play along."

"Play along?" Tomi asked.

Maeve shrugged. "They might be a backward settlement without much to offer, but we could always use cheap labor and taxes. Don't you agree?" Maeve asked, raising one eyebrow at Tomi.

"Of course, Madam Mayor," he acknowledged with a twinge of sympathy for the Primes. If they took the Mayor's offer, they'd become little more than indentured servants, but that wasn't his problem.

"Now. To the real reason you're here," Maeve said, straightening up.

Ah. Here it is, Tomi thought. He tossed back the last of the brandy. *I might as well enjoy the good stuff while I can. I have a bad feeling about this.*

"We recently lost contact with a research facility to the North. It went dark, and despite our best efforts, we have not been able to reestablish communications," Maeve explained.

"I heard about it," Tomi said. "You sent a team out at the same time we left, didn't you?"

"We did," Maeve said. "We sent the Primes, equipped with the necessary supplies to reach the facility and investigate the problem. If the facility is lost, they are to retrieve any research and survivors."

"May I ask why you didn't send my team and me? The likelihood of success would've been much higher if you had," Tomi said.

"I didn't want to risk a high-value asset, and the Primes owe us for the supplies we've given them. I thought it a suitable way for them to repay us."

And if they die in the process, you wouldn't care since they're not your people. No squealing from the opposition parties either, Tomi thought with shrewd accuracy.

While he might be a mere soldier, he kept his ear to the ground, and he knew the Mayor was on shaky ground. After a couple of recent setbacks, she couldn't afford to lose any more support. The opposition circled her like sharks, waiting for her blood to chum the waters.

"What does any of this have to do with my crew or me?" Tomi asked. "I assume I'm here for a reason."

"You assume correctly," Maeve said, her voice taking on a sharp edge. "Since the Primes departed on their quest, certain information has come to light."

"Oh?" Tomi said, cocking his head.

"It appears the Primes have friends in Vancouver. One in particular called Jessica Gates."

"I've heard of her. She's a freelancer, and a good one too," Tomi said.

"She's more than good. She's excellent. I've employed her in the past, including on the last scouting mission to find other settlements. I won't bore you with the details, but she found her way to Prime City and made friends during her stay. The same friends she chose to accompany on their mission."

Tomi nodded, slowly putting the pieces of the puzzle together. "I see. She joined the Primes."

"That's right, and normally, I wouldn't care. She's an expert in the field, and her help greatly increases their chances of success."

"But?" Tomi asked.

"But, she didn't go alone. She recruited backup in the form of Ronan Gay and his team," Maeve said, jumping up from her chair. "I do not trust this Ronan, and I was proven right."

"What happened?"

"The day they left, a woman called Lila broke into my office and stole sensitive information about the research facility to the North. Information not meant for unauthorized people."

"Let me guess. This Lila is part of Ronan's team?" Tomi said.

"That is correct, and I fear they plan to use that information

8

to their advantage. Either by selling it to the highest bidder or by blackmailing me."

"And you want me to retrieve it for you?" Tomi asked.

"Exactly," Maeve said. She pinned him to the spot with a fierce gaze. "But that isn't all. My daughter went with them, and I want her back, alive and whole."

"Your daughter?" Tomi said, taken aback. "Why would she join them on such a dangerous mission?"

Maeve sighed. "She and Jessica worked together on the scouting mission and became good friends. Also, she has a misplaced sense of adventure. You know how youngsters are. They think they're invincible."

Tomi winced, remembering the time his own children were teenagers. Rebellious, difficult, and all-knowing, it was a miracle they made it to adulthood in one piece. He was grateful that particular period in his life was over. "What about the Primes?"

"I don't care about them. Whether they live or die is of little concern to me," Maeve said with a dismissive wave. "The only thing I care about is that research... and my daughter. Do you understand?"

"Yes, Madam Mayor," Tomi said, though he found it strange that she'd mentioned the research first and her daughter second. *Does her own flesh and blood mean so little to her?*

"You leave first thing tomorrow morning," Maeve added.

"Yes, Madam Mayor," Tomi replied, calculating the hours he had left to spend at home with Marie. It wasn't a lot, and he heaved an inward sigh. *So much for that beer.*

"You can choose your team and take whatever equipment you need. You have my full backing on this mission," Maeve said. "Plus, there's a promotion waiting for you if you succeed."

9

"A promotion?"

"Yes, I'll promote you to full Captain with all the associated perks, privileges, and pay."

"Thank you, Madam Mayor," Tomi said, surprised. Being promoted to the rank of Captain was no small thing. It showed him how desperate she was, and he realized there was more at stake than she was letting on. "I appreciate it."

"That is all. You may go now. I imagine you have a lot to arrange before morning," Maeve said, moving to stand behind her desk.

"Yes, Madam Mayor. Indeed I do," Tomi said. As he walked toward the door, a sharp word brought him to a halt.

"Lieutenant!"

Tomi stopped in his tracks. "Yes?"

"Do not fail me."

"I won't, Madam Mayor."

"If you do, don't bother coming back," she added, her voice like ice.

"Yes, Madam Mayor," Tomi said, gritting his teeth. He did not like being threatened or bullied, especially by a politician.

He shot her a final look before leaving the office, imprinting the image of her on his brain: the glittering eyes, white teeth, and sharp nails.

For a brief moment, his perspective shifted, and he glimpsed the darkness beneath the polished veneer. She was a monster in disguise, a leech feeding on the people of Vancouver and their trade partners. If allowed to remain in power, her ambition would grow until it consumed them all.

The realization hit him with the force of a sledgehammer, and he fled from the building and burst out into the open. The cold air cleared his mind and allowed him to think. Before him lay a critical decision, one that could change his entire life. *But first, I have a mission to fulfill.*

Chapter 1

Rogue picked her way through the swamp, jumping from one grassy tussock to another. Her foot slipped, one boot landing in a deep puddle of brown, stagnant water. Wrinkling her nose, she raised the offending limb in the air and shook off the worst of the gunk. "Ugh. That is gross. What is that smell?"

"It smells like rotten eggs," Jessica agreed, navigating the damp terrain a few feet away. She jumped from one patch of dry ground to another, her arms cartwheeling for balance.

"It's like something died out here," Imogen said with an expression of disgust.

Silence fell across the group as her words sunk in, an awful awareness of what it might mean and what they might find out in the watery wastes.

"He's not dead," Ronan said, his tone flat. "Spook is alive, and we'll find him."

"Oh, I'm sorry. I didn't mean to imply—" Imogen began.

"Just drop it," Ronan said.

"But I—"

"You heard him," Lila said. "Just drop it."

Imogen flashed Rogue a look of desperation, her gaze a silent plea for help.

"Sorry," Rogue mimed, shrugging her shoulders. There

wasn't much she or anyone else could say or do. Nothing but find the missing Spook. Either dead or alive. The latter, preferably.

Ronan was convinced that Spook had wandered off and gotten lost during the night. He was not dead, just lost, and they needed to find him. Of that, he was certain.

Rogue wasn't so sure. Why would Spook wander off? Alone and in the dark? It didn't make sense, and she was afraid something had happened to the boy. It was not a pleasant thought. As annoying as he was, he was part of the group, and they needed him.

With a sigh, Rogue focused on her footing. The ground was treacherous, and the last thing she needed was to land in a puddle of quicksand or a sucking bog. Mud squelched beneath her feet, and a dozen mosquitoes buzzed around her ears. She waved them away with zero success and muttered, "I hate this place."

"What's that, my love?" Seth asked, stealing up behind her.

"Don't do that!" Rogue cried, nearly jumping out of her skin. "I thought you were...."

"You thought I was a what? A croc?" he asked with a teasing smile.

"It's not funny," Rogue said, dropping her voice to a low whisper. "Spook is missing, and I'm afraid something got him."

The smile dropped from Seth's face, and he nodded. "It's possible."

"And I'm afraid for myself too," Rogue admitted. "I mean, who knows what's out there, lurking in the mud?"

"It's okay to be scared. I'm scared, too," Seth said.

"You are?" she asked, throwing him a dubious look.

"Of course. Have you seen the size of the crocodiles out

13

here? They're monsters!" he said, waving a hand around. "And they could be anywhere."

Rogue's heart jumped into her throat. "Don't say that. How am I supposed to continue the search now?"

Seth shrugged. "We have to. Because if we don't find Spook or some sign of what happened to him, Ronan won't continue the journey."

"I know. He's very loyal toward his teammates," Rogue said. "I just hope that loyalty extends to us, as well."

"That remains to be seen," Seth said, his tone guarded.

"You don't think he's on our side?" Rogue asked.

"He's on someone's side, that's for sure."

Rogue frowned. "I don't like this. I don't like any of it. This so-called mission. This horrible place. Spook's disappearance. It's all wrong."

"I know, but we didn't have a choice. It was either this or Prime starves," Seth said.

"I realize that," Rogue said, flashing him a sharp look. "But it's still wrong."

Silence fell, filled only by the noxious buzzing of insects. Rogue waved at a cloud of midges that rose from a nearby bog. They swarmed around her and Seth, feasting on their exposed skin.

Rogue tried to wave them away but without success. They were everywhere at once. A couple even flew up her nose, and she sneezed so hard she thought she would pass out. "Atchoo, atchoo, atchoo. Ugh! Atchoo!"

"Come on," Seth cried, grabbing her hand. He dragged her away from the spot until they reached a clearing free from the bloodsucking mites. There they paused to catch their breath.

"Ugh, that was nasty," Rogue said, hacking and coughing.

Tears poured down her cheeks, and her nose itched like crazy.

Seth handed her a piece of cloth. "Here, blow your nose."

She took the rag and did as he suggested. Finally, the itching passed, and her eyes stopped watering. Able to see again, she looked around, and alarm spiked within her chest. "Where are the others?"

"I don't know," Seth admitted, turning in a slow circle.

"What do you mean you don't know?"

"Well, do you see them anywhere?"

"We lost them?" Rogue cried, aghast.

"Lost is a strong word."

Rogue arched an eyebrow. "Really? You think this is funny?"

"We'll find them. You'll see," Seth said with an air of bravado.

"Alright. Go ahead," Rogue said, waving a hand.

Seth took the lead and wound his way through the swampy terrain with an air of confidence that she guessed he didn't feel. But she followed him anyway simply because she had no idea where to go either.

"Ronan? Jessica? Bear!" Seth called every few seconds.

There was no reply.

Rogue swallowed hard, her eyes swiveling in their sockets. Every step sent a prickle of fear down her spine. The swamp was not the place for warm, breathing creatures. It was a place for scales, spines, slithering tongues, and ragged teeth.

A twig snapped nearby, and she froze to the spot, unable to move. Her breathing grew shallow in her chest while she searched for the source of the noise. A rustle in the trees sent her pulse through the roof, and she reached for the handgun at her waist. "Seth. There is something here."

Seth paused, his posture stiff. "Where?"

With a quivering hand, she pointed in the direction of the

sound. "Over there, I think. It's hard to tell."

"Don't move," Seth warned, removing his rifle from his back. He checked the load and walked forward, placing each foot with care. A clump of trees loomed overhead, and he stepped into its shadow.

The leaves overhead quivered when he got close, and he stopped in his tracks. Raising the gun, he studied the trees. "I can't see anything."

"That doesn't mean there's nothing there."

"I know."

A branch snapped.

"Be careful," Rogue said, aiming her gun at the foliage. Whatever was inside, it was about to get a mouthful of bullets.

The leaves burst apart, and a flock of flyers erupted from within its dark confines. Their leathery wings beat the air, and they swirled overhead, a vortex of sharp beaks and claws. Disturbed within their nest by the two-legged strangers, they attacked in a bid to defend their territory.

They were smaller than most Pterosaurs, and Rogue guessed they were fish-eaters, preying on the fish and small lizards that spawned within the vast swampy inland sea. That didn't mean much, however. With a wingspan of several feet and a razor-sharp beak, they were nothing to sniff at. Plus, they had numbers on their side.

"Rogue, get down," Seth yelled.

Rogue threw herself to the side and covered her head with her arms. Talons raked across her back and tugged at her hair. Harsh caws filled her ears, and she rolled over to escape the snapping beaks that tore at her flesh.

Gunshots exploded inside the clearing, and she dared a quick glance at Seth. He aimed and shot with cool precision, not missing a beat. Several flyers crashed to the ground, their blood like puffs of crimson mist in the air. Their bodies convulsed in the mud, the membranes on their wings stretched taut before they sagged into death.

Rogue turned toward Seth, determined to join him, but a Pterosaur launched itself at her with a shrill shriek of rage. She kicked at it with both feet and crawled away, not caring where she went. Mud squelched beneath her elbows, and a patch of slimy moss smoothed her path.

The flyer followed, tearing at her boots and denim pants. She cried out when its beak ripped through the material and sliced into her calf muscle. Hot pain lanced up the limb and raced through her nerve-endings until her hair stood on end. "Ah, shit, that hurts!"

More than a little pissed, Rogue rolled over and aimed her gun at the Pterosaur. It stormed across the ground. With its wings folded back, it waddled toward her like an old man on crutches, except it was much faster.

Too fast.

Before she knew it, the creature was upon her, its beak clacking at her face. With a scream of horror, Rogue pulled the trigger. A splash of warm blood hit her in the face, and the flyer crashed on top of her, dead. Its head was blown away, leaking fluids and brains onto her shirt.

"Ack," Rogue yelled, shoving the corpse aside.

She rolled over and gagged, the taste of metal strong in her mouth. Once she could breathe, she jumped to her feet and looked around. Wounded flyers flapped around on the ground, their plaintive squawks painful to hear. The rest of the flock decided they'd had enough and made good their escape.

"Are you hurt?" Seth asked once the area was clear.

"It's nothing serious," Rogue said, though it hurt to walk with her wounded leg. "A few cuts and scrapes."

"Me too," Seth said with a look of relief. He glanced at the wounded Pterosaurs and sighed. "Let's take care of them. No need to let them suffer."

Rogue nodded, removing the machete from her belt. She walked toward the nearest wounded creature and ended its misery with a quick chop of the blade. A second flyer struggled in a puddle of mud, and she headed toward it. As she raised the machete in the air, the Pterosaur summoned a final burst of energy and attacked.

It bowled her over, and she fell into a thick patch of vegetation. The machete flew out of her hand, and she raised her arms to fend off the creature. But it sagged to the ground, the life fading from its eyes.

"Are you okay?" Seth called.

"Yeah, I'm fine," Rogue replied, looking around. She was stuck in a clump of bushes, her clothes damp and smeared with mud. Rolling over, she crawled forward but wrinkled her nose when her hand hit something slimy. "Ugh, what is that?"

She looked down, and for a moment, the world ceased to turn. Vomit rose up her throat, and she yanked her hand away. Rubbing it on her jeans, she scrambled backward, screaming at the top of her lungs.

"What is it?" Seth cried, rushing over.

With a trembling finger, Rogue pointed at the object she'd discovered. It was a head, partially submerged in the mud and covered with leaves. The eyes stared vacantly into the distance, and bloody froth leaked from the lips. "I think... I think I found Spook."

18

Chapter 2

Seth helped her to her feet, and Rogue clung to him, unable to take her eyes off the grizzly sight of Spook's head. It didn't even look like him. Not anymore. Tendrils of flesh and sinew hung from his severed neck, and his eyes looked like curdled milk. She swallowed hard as the urge to hurl kicked in. "Where's the body?"

"That's a good question," Seth said, his voice grim.

Yells and footsteps sounded as people stumbled into the clearing.

"What's going on?" Ronan asked. "We heard gunshots."

"Is everyone okay?" Jessica said, slightly out of breath.

"Oh my God!" Imogen cried, spotting the decapitated head first. "Is that... Spook?"

She turned away and vomited into the nearest bush, her slender body convulsing as it expelled the contents of her stomach.

Rogue pressed a hand to her lips, willing her stomach into submission. *Please, don't hurl. Please, don't hurl. Not here. Not now.*

Ronan stared at the girl, his brow furrowed. "What are you talking about?"

"Over there," Daniel said, spotting the severed head. He

pointed at the spot, and Ronan's gaze followed.

In an instant, his expression changed from mild alarm to shock, surprise, anger, and finally, grief. "Spook? It can't be." He walked forward, his steps slow and reluctant. "What happened to you?"

Daniel followed, sticking close to Ronan. He sighed as he studied the head. "It must've been a croc."

"A crocodile?" Lila asked, her voice shrill. She backed away from the clearing, her eyes swiveling in their sockets.

"The wound is ragged. It's not a clean-cut," Daniel said.

"Is it still here?" Lila said. "It's still here. Watching us. It has to be!"

"What's that?" Imogen added, straightening up. She wiped her mouth and shivered. "Please, don't say that."

"I can feel its beady eyes on me right now," Lila said, clearly close to losing her nerves.

"Calm down, for fuck's sake," Jessica said, rolling her eyes. "It's not here."

"Oh yeah? How do you know that?" Lila cried.

"Because, if it were here, it would've attacked already," Jessica said.

"I don't believe you."

"Then let me prove it." Jessica removed her rifle from her back and checked the load. With the weapon ready to shoot, she walked around the edges of the clearing. After doing a full circuit, she paused. "See? Nothing."

"It could still be around," Lila said, turning sullen.

"I hope not," Imogen added.

"Shut up. All of you," Ronan said. He glared at Lila and Imogen. "Spook is dead, and all you care about is yourselves."

"I'm sorry," Imogen whispered, tears brimming in her eyes.

Lila said nothing, but the look she gave Ronan was hostile.

Silence fell across the clearing, thick and heavy. Rogue held on to Seth, not sure what to do or say. It was an impossible situation, and she had no idea how to react. The overwhelming emotion she felt was horror. Horror and pity for Spook. *What an awful way to die.*

Finally, Ronan broke the silence. "Go back to camp, everyone."

"What about you?" Jessica asked.

"I'm going to look for the rest of him, and then I'm going to bury him," Ronan said.

"Alone?" Jessica said.

"He was my responsibility, and I'll do what's right by him," Ronan replied, his expression tight. "The rest of you can wait at camp."

"I'll help you look for his body," Daniel said.

"No," Ronan said.

"He was part of the team, Boss. Part of my team," Daniel said, folding his arms across his chest. "I'm not letting you do this alone."

"Me neither," Lila said.

"You?" Jessica said with a snort. "Aren't you afraid of the crocodile?"

"Screw you, princess. Spook was one of us," Lila said, her eyes glittering.

"We'll all stay," Seth said, speaking up for the first time. "We'll find him faster if we work together."

"Fine," Ronan said. "But keep out of my way. All of you."

"We'll need shovels," Jessica said. "Bear, and I will fetch some from the trucks."

"Take Imogen with you," Rogue suggested. "She doesn't have

21

to be here."

Imogen shot Rogue a grateful smile, her cheeks pale. "Thanks."

Jessica, Bear, and Imogen marched back to camp, and the rest began the search for Spook's body. It didn't take long. Ronan and Daniel found the rest of him a few yards away from the head.

It wasn't a pretty sight, and Rogue nearly lost her lunch for the second time that day. He was missing an arm and half a leg. His stomach was torn open, the entrails eaten out until only a gaping maw remained.

"It was definitely a crocodile," Daniel said.

Ronan didn't reply. Instead, he stared at the body, a muscle in his jaw ticking.

"Ronan," Daniel said. "Ronan!"

Ronan stirred. "What?"

"We have to bury him and get back to camp before the crocodile returns for the rest of its meal."

"Let it. I'll be waiting," Ronan said.

"Don't be stupid. It's too dangerous. It'll be dark in a couple of hours," Daniel said.

"I don't care."

"Ronan, please," Daniel said, tugging Ronan's arm.

Ronan yanked free from his grip. "Leave me alone."

"Boss…"

"Don't you get it? This is my fault. I'm to blame. I should've watched him, protected him, and I didn't," Ronan cried. "All that's left now is to get revenge!"

"On a dumb animal that doesn't know any better?" Daniel said, incredulous.

Rogue watched the exchange from a distance. Finally, she

could stand no more and stepped forward. "You're right, Ronan. Spook was your responsibility, and you failed him."

"Excuse me?" Ronan said, turning to face her.

"That's what you want to hear, right?" Rogue asked.

Ronan gritted his teeth. "What's your point?"

"My point is, you failed Spook, but you're also the leader of three more people. Daniel, Lila, and Nigel. Or have you forgotten?" She gestured at each person as she named them, and they all watched Ronan for his reply.

"I haven't forgotten them. How could I?" Ronan said, waving at them. "They're right here."

"That's right. They're here, and they're also your responsibility," Rogue pointed out. "They're your team. Right, guys?"

Lila nodded. "We're a team."

"Always, Boss."

"We'll miss Spook, but we're still here," Nigel said.

Ronan stared at each of them in turn before he nodded. "You're right. I apologize for my behavior."

"It's understandable," Nigel said.

"But we need to hurry," Lila added with a shiver.

"Let's gather Spook's remains and pay our respects," Daniel said.

"Alright," Ronan agreed, and together, they tackled the unpleasant job.

Jessica and Bear returned shortly after that with a couple of shovels and a blanket, much to Rogue's relief. "Let's do this," she whispered to Seth.

"Agreed. The sooner we're done, the better," Seth said. "We're too exposed out here."

The men took turns digging the grave while Jessica and Rogue wrapped the remains in the blanket. Lila volunteered

23

to stand watch, unable to look at what was left of Spook, and Rogue didn't blame her. It was an ugly job, and she hated seeing Spook like that. *He was so young. That could've been me.*

The thought made her shudder, and she worked faster. Afterward, she washed her bloody hands in a puddle of muddy water, scrubbing furiously to get the rusty stains off her skin.

"We're done," Seth said, standing back from the edge of the grave.

Ronan and Daniel buried Spook, and Nigel cleared his throat. "Should I say a prayer? I don't think Spook was religious."

"Say it anyway," Ronan said. "He deserves a proper burial."

"Alright," Nigel agreed.

***

Our heavenly Father, we pray that You will find mercy on the soul of Spook. We pray that his soul may find peace with his unexpected death, and that he has lived a good life and did his best serving his family, workplace, and loved ones while he was on earth. We also earnestly seek the forgiveness of all his sins and shortcomings. May he find assurance that his family will remain strong and steadfast in serving the Lord as he moves forward in his journey to eternal life with Christ, his Lord, and Savior. Dear Father, take His soul into Your kingdom and let perpetual light shine upon him; may he rest in peace. Amen.

***

"Thank you, Nigel," Ronan said.

"Well, it's the least I could do for him," Nigel said.

"Let's go," Ronan said, turning away. He trooped to camp, followed closely by the rest of the group.

Along the way, Seth paused to grab a Pterosaur corpse. He tied a rope around its wings and carried it by the feet. "We've got fresh meat for dinner."

"Really?" Rogue asked, wrinkling her nose. "Flyers are so stringy and bony."

"It's still real meat," he said.

Rogue shrugged. Food was food, and she couldn't afford to be picky. As they walked, she stuck close to Seth, wondering what else the swamp hid within its damp, slimy depths. "I really hate this place."

"You and me both," Seth agreed, taking her hand. "Don't worry. We'll be out of here soon enough."

"Man, I hope so," Rogue replied with a final look over her shoulder.

The swamp gazed back, a menacing forest knee-deep in stagnant, murky water, filled with all sorts of creatures, and none of them friendly. The hair on the back of her neck rose, and she quickened her pace. *The sooner we get out of this place, the better.*

Chapter 3

The walk back to camp was short, but it was too late to travel further. The search for Spook, the discovery of his body, and the burial had taken most of the day, and it was late afternoon already. Traveling in the dark was impossible. They'd never be able to navigate the bogs, stretches of water, and patches of quicksand.

"Settle down, folks. We're spending the night," Ronan said.

"Great," Rogue said with a groan, not thrilled at the idea of spending another night in the same place Spook got ambushed.

"Sorry, babes," Seth said, giving her a reassuring hug.

"I keep thinking about it," she said in a low whisper.

"About what?"

"Spook's last moments. It must've been awful. Getting eaten by a crocodile," she said with a shudder.

"I don't think he suffered," Seth said.

"No?"

"You've seen those things, right? From a distance?"

"Yeah," she replied, thinking back. It had been quite a shock the first time she saw a crocodile. Somehow, she'd failed to imagine the sheer size and scope of the beasts. They were monstrous. There was no other word for it.

"Spook wouldn't have had much time to feel anything. One

bite, and he was a goner," Seth said.

"Yeah, I suppose you're right."

"Come on. Let's get you patched up," Seth said.

"I'm okay," Rogue mumbled but allowed him to treat her wounds. They weren't serious, primarily scrapes and bruises. But the cut on her leg was deep and needed a couple of stitches. He disinfected and bandaged the wound before declaring her done.

"Your turn," she said, reaching for the med-kit. Seth likewise suffered from minor cuts and contusions, none of them severe.

"Right," Seth said when she was done. "Let's make supper. It'll pass the time, and a hot meal is exactly what everyone needs right now."

"Okay," she agreed.

"Besides, we've got fresh meat, and we can't let that go to waste."

"True, but you're doing the butchering," Rogue said, pulling a face.

"Deal."

Together, Rogue and Seth prepared a simple dinner of Pteradon steaks fried with wild onions, garlic, and herbs. Afterward, they prepared a pot of coffee and settled down around the fire. Despite the good meal, the atmosphere was grim, and the silence was thick and heavy. It didn't take long for people to make their excuses.

"I'll take the first watch," Ronan said.

"Be careful," Rogue said.

"I'll be fine." He stepped outside the light cast by the fire.

The darkness swallowed him whole, and Rogue stared at the spot, worried despite herself. To her, the swamp was a sucking hole filled with terrifying creatures waiting to pounce. No one was safe around it or in it. No one.

"I'm off to bed. Thanks for the food," Lila said, jumping to her feet.

"Me too," Daniel said.

"Good night, everyone," Imogen echoed.

Only Nigel lingered, his expression stark. "He was a good boy, Spook. A little weird, perhaps, but he had a good heart."

"We know, and we're sorry," Jessica said.

"And he was so clever," Nigel continued. "He knew stuff I could never dream off."

"A real nerd," Rogue said with a small laugh. "In a good way, of course."

"I'm going to miss him," Nigel said with a shake of the head.

"Does he have any family?" Jessica asked.

"A mom and a younger sister."

Jessica whistled. "That's tough. Will they be taken care of?"

"Of course. Ronan will see to it. He won't let them want for anything."

"I'm glad," Jessica said.

"Well, that's it for me," Nigel said, getting up. "See you tomorrow."

"Goodnight," Rogue murmured, feeling a pang of sorrow for the man. It was apparent he'd cared about Spook. More than any of them had suspected.

Silence fell across the group, and she fidgeted on the spot. To lighten the mood, she turned to Jessica. "Tell us how you met Ronan. You never did tell us."

"There's not much to tell," Jessica said with a wary glance at Bear.

He eyed her before giving a brisk nod. "I don't mind. We're friends now. Tell the story."

"Yes, please, Jessica. Tell us," Imogen pleaded.

"Alright. If you insist," Jessica said, staring into the distance.

Rogue smiled, eager to hear the story. It was sure to be a good one, and they could all use the distraction.

"Settle in, guys. It's a long one."

"We've got time," Bear said, his chest rumbling. He shifted his bulk into a more comfortable position and poured himself another cup of coffee.

"Go ahead, Jessica," Seth said, taking Rogue's hand.

Imogen clapped her hands with a happy squeal. "Ooh, I can't wait!"

"It happened four years ago, during one of the coldest winters on record. The Mayor, Imogen's mom, contracted us to scout a section of land earmarked for mining. A party of geologists had discovered a rich iron deposit in the area, but they also suffered severe losses through predator attacks. We, Ronan and I, were sent in to determine the severity of the problem and come up with a solution."

"Why you?" Rogue asked.

"My father was a renowned big-game hunter in his day, and the Shift didn't change that. To him, all creatures were the same, no matter their size. You simply had to know how to hunt them. As an only child, he taught me everything he knew, and I took over the business after he died. I soon expanded into scouting, retrieving, discovery, hunting problem dinosaurs, and clearing areas needed for expansion. Ronan, though more of a mercenary with his military background, offered the same services, and we were both contracted for the job."

"And? What did you find?" Imogen asked, jumping up and down.

"Who's telling the story?" Jessica asked with a raised eyebrow.

"You or me?"

"Sorry," Imogen mumbled, striving, and failing, to look contrite.

"Anyway. At first, Ronan and I didn't get along. We considered ourselves rivals, and things got quite tense between us. I was on the verge of quitting when we spotted tracks near the camp. "Tarbosaurus tracks."

Rogue gasped, unable to help herself. When Jessica paused, she waved her on. "Sorry. Continue, please."

"Alright. But no more interruptions. Got it?" Jessica said, looking from one person to the next.

"Got it," they answered.

Jessica smiled and leaned closer to the fire, letting the glow wash across her face. "Good. Because you don't want to miss the next part of the story."

A log collapsed into the coals, and sparks flew up into the night sky. A slight breeze whistled through the camp, and the sounds of the swamp grew distant as Jessica continued her tale.

Chapter 4 - Jessica

Dawn was still a long way off when Jessica slipped out of her tent. Around her, the camp began to stir as early risers like her went about their chores. The cook stoked the fire in the middle of the circle of tents, and the smell of coffee filled the air. A couple of guards walked past, relieving those on night duty, and a donkey brayed in the distance. It was a day much like any other. Except it wasn't.

"Right, let's go over this one more time," Jessica muttered, sitting down on the wooden stump that served as a stool.

She opened her backpack and checked the contents: A water canteen, three days' worth of rations, a first-aid kit, spare ammunition, a knife, a length of cord, spare socks, a comb, and a bedroll. Satisfied, she closed the flap and set the pack aside.

Next, she checked the load on her .416 Rigby Mauser, a gift from her late father, and slung it across her shoulder. Though it only sported four bullets, it had massive stopping power at close range.

She also carried a .480 Ruger as a backup weapon on one hip and a machete on the other. Her unruly hair was drawn back into a tight bun, and her khaki pants, jacket, and hiking boots were strong, lightweight, and durable. A cotton t-shirt, socks, and underwear allowed her skin to breathe and wicked away excess moisture. A woolen beanie was the final touch. It kept her scalp and ears warm, preventing her from losing too much body heat in the cold.

As she worked, she remained alert and aware of her surroundings. It was the one thing her dad hammered into her brain as a child. *Never let your guard down. No matter how safe you think you are, anything can happen.*

His voice rang in her head, and she could almost see him again. The familiar scent of cologne and gun powder tingled her nostrils, and fierce longing seized hold of her heart. It'd been scarcely a year since he passed, and at times, she thought the grief would cripple her. But now was not the time to mourn her father. Not when she had to contend with a dangerous man-eating predator and a moron of epic proportions.

"Hey, Jess. I'm glad to see you're awake," a voice called. "I thought for sure I'd have to drag your ass out of bed."

"Speaking of morons," Jessica muttered below her breath. She looked up into the face of Ronan, her supposed partner on this expedition and a constant thorn in her side. If it weren't for the discovery of tracks the day before, she'd have quit just to be rid of him.

"First of all, it's Jessica. Not Jess. Secondly, if you dare lay a finger on my ass, you're losing it," she said, removing the machete from its sheath.

"Tsk, tsk. Someone got up on the wrong side of the bed," Ronan said, raising both hands to ward her off.

"Don't test me," Jessica warned, pointing the blade at him.

"Whatever. Are you ready to go? Time's a-wasting," Ronan said.

"I'm ready," she replied, standing up. She slung her bag onto her back before securing her rifle and putting the machete away.

"What's with all the baggage?" Ronan asked. "We won't be gone that long."

"I believe in being prepared."

Ronan shrugged. "Your funeral."

He set off, and she noticed he carried only his weapons and a canteen—nothing else.

Huh. He'd better hope nothing goes wrong, or he'll be sorry, she thought with a smirk. *I might be paranoid, but I'm never caught unawares.*

Two men and a woman joined them on the way out. All three were guards who'd volunteered the night before. Jessica didn't know them and didn't think they were needed, but Ronan agreed before she could object.

"We can always use the help," he'd said with an affable smile.

Jessica snorted at the memory. Armed with knives and low-caliber rifles, the guards wouldn't be able to help them even if they tried. Only she and Ronan were properly armed for the creatures that lurked beyond the camp. At best, the volunteers could be used as bait or cannon fodder.

They set out on foot and headed toward the spot where the carnivore tracks had been seen the day before. Moving fast, they made good time and reached the area just as the sun showed its face on the horizon.

"The tracks should be around here somewhere," Ronan said.

"You three stay put," Jessica told the guards. The last thing she needed was for a bunch of rookies to trample the evidence.

She took slow, careful steps and swept the ground with a keen gaze. Her senses were on high alert, aware that whatever had made the tracks could still be around. It didn't take long to pick up the trail, and she called Ronan. "Over here."

Jessica dropped to one knee and traced the footprint with one finger. It was still fresh, the edges crisp, and the earth without blemish. No insects had wandered across the trail, and only a thin layer of dew covered it. "It was made recently."

"Yes, sometime during the night," he agreed.

"I thought they found these yesterday afternoon?"

Ronan cast around and pointed to more tracks. "These are older."

Jessica walked over and noted the fainter footprints. "That means the creature returned to this site after the tracks were found yesterday."

"Yes, but why?"

"This is most likely part of its territory," Jessica said with a frown.

"Probably, and the camp is nearby. No wonder they've been attacked," Ronan said. "It's an easy food source right within its domain."

Jessica nodded. "That leaves us with two choices. Move the camp or kill it."

"We can't move the camp. It's right next to the iron deposits."

"That means we have to kill it," Jessica affirmed. "The question is, what are we dealing with?"

"It's not as large as a T-Rex but close, judging by the tracks," Ronan mused.

"Not a Gorgosaurus or Carnotaurus then," Jessica said. "Or even an Albertosaurus."

"It's heavy. Look how deep that print sinks into the ground. Four, maybe five tons?" Ronan said. "And about ten meters long if you look at the stride."

"Tarbosaurus?" Jessica asked.

"You think so? I haven't seen one in years," Ronan mused.

"It fits with the evidence."

"Damn. That means we're in for a rough ride," Ronan said.

"A Tarbosaurus? What's that? I've never heard of it," one of the three guards asked.

"A Tarbosaurus is a slightly smaller version of the T-rex," Ronan said.

"You say it's smaller?" the man asked with a hopeful look.

"Not enough so you'd notice," Ronan replied. "Let's just say the Tarbosaurus is the T-rex's younger cousin, slightly smaller but twice as mean."

"That's right," Jessica said, standing up. "So if you want to chicken out, now's the time."

The trio looked at each other, suddenly unsure of their place on the team. Hunting a rogue dino alongside two renowned big-game hunters was one thing but going after a beast like that was tantamount to suicide.

"I'm not afraid. I'm staying," the woman said first.

"So am I," the other guard said.

Outvoted, the third guard who spoke earlier opted to stay as well.

"Go on then?" Ronan prompted. "Seeing as we might die today, I might as well know your names."

"I'm Lucia. That is Dean, and that's Frodo," the woman said.

"Frodo?" Ronan said with a smirk.

Lucia shrugged. "It's a nickname."

The third guard, or Frodo, blushed. "I've got very hairy feet."

"Really? Now that's something I've got to see," Ronan cried.

Jessica threw her hands in the air. "Are we here to hunt or gawk at hairy feet?"

"I guess we'd better get on with it before Jess here has a fit,"

Ronan said. "She's no fun at all, unlike her dad. I heard he was a jolly old chap before he croaked."

As fast as lightning, Jessica whipped the machete from its sheath and pressed the razor-sharp blade to Ronan's neck, right above the carotid artery. "My name is Jessica. Only my friends get to call me Jess, and you are not my friend."

Ronan paled, and he slowly raised both hands in the air. "Whoa there. There's no need for violence."

"What gives you the right to talk about my father like that, you piece of shit?" Jessica hissed with bared teeth.

"I didn't mean it like that, okay? It was just a joke."

"You and your silly little jokes. Well, this time, you've gone too far. Give me one good reason not to kill you right here."

"Err, I'm good-looking, sexy, and useful?" Ronan quipped, but his expression was strained. "I can be very useful."

Jessica growled. "More jokes."

"Besides, you're not that good-looking," Lucia said. "Or sexy."

"Hey! Whose side are you on?" Ronan asked.

"Hers. She's got the knife," Lucia replied.

"Yeah, I'd gut you like a fish if you spoke about my family like that," Dean said with a shrug.

"Frodo? Help me out here," Ronan pleaded.

"Sorry, but I'm with them," Frodo said, his blue eyes wide and innocent.

"Traitors," Ronan muttered.

"Just say you're sorry," Lucia prompted.

"Me? Apologize?" Ronan asked, aghast.

"There's always a first time for everything," Dean said.

"It was just a joke," Ronan said. "I didn't even know her father."

"Exactly. Say you're sorry," Lucia prompted.

Ronan opened his mouth, hesitated, closed it again, then sighed. "I...."

"Argh, forget it," Jessica cried. "This is a waste of time."

She pulled back, leaving a red line on Ronan's throat. A bead of blood welled up, and he touched it with his fingers. Staring at the crimson smear, he said, "You cut me. I can't believe you cut me."

Jessica leveled the machete at him. "Next time you talk about my father, I'll do more than cut you. I'll kill you. Got that?"

"Got it," Ronan grumbled. "Can we hunt some Tarbosaurus now?"

"Lead the way," Jessica said, waving a hand.

"Why me?" Ronan asked with a look of suspicion.

"That way you can get eaten first," Jessica said with a fake smile.

"Fine. If that's what it will take to put a smile on your face, so be it," Ronan said, flashing her a mean look.

He picked up the trail and struck out with the rest following close on his heels. Moving with care, Ronan steered clear of any trees and bushes. He stuck to the open and kept watch for danger, but it wasn't long before they hit a roadblock.

A big one.

"Holy shit," Ronan said, whistling.

"What in hell's name is that?" Lucia said.

Jessica stopped in her tracks and eyed the scene ahead with a sense of trepidation. A field of grass swayed in the wind, the beige stalks easily reaching eight feet in length, taller than any of them. She looked from side to side, but there was no end to the sea of grass. No way around it. "That is trouble."

"No kidding, but that's where the tracks lead," Ronan said.

"I know, but we won't be able to see a thing in there," Jessica added. "We'll be blind."

"I don't see any other option, and we have to get the job done," Ronan said, his mouth set in a stubborn line. "Come on, guys. Are you with me?"

Lucia didn't answer, her expression doubtful.

"You want us to go in there?" Dean asked.

"I don't want to go in there," Frodo said, backing away. "Are you crazy?"

"Come on, you bunch of pussies. You signed up for this, remember?" Ronan said.

"I didn't sign up for that," Dean said, pointing at the ocean of grass.

Ronan changed tactics. "Come on, Jess. I mean Jessica. If we don't kill that dinosaur, it'll come back to camp, and more innocent people will suffer. This is what we were hired for."

Jessica hesitated, aware she was being manipulated. Going after the Tarbosaurus was tantamount to suicide. Still, she didn't want anyone else to die, and she had been hired for the job. *If we leave now, I might have blood on my hands tomorrow.*

"So? What will it be?" Ronan prompted.

After a couple of seconds, she gave a brisk nod. "Alright. Let's do this."

"Yes!" Ronan said with a grin, his blood lust up.

"On one condition," Jessica interrupted.

"What's that?"

"I'll take the lead on this expedition. Not you," Jessica said. "You do what I say when I say it. Got that?"

"I shall be the perfect gentleman," Ronan said. He stepped aside and waved at the wall of grass with a fancy flourish. "After you, Milady."

Jessica rolled her eyes, already regretting her decision.

Studying the group, she was able to fully appreciate her folly. *I'm now responsible for the lives of four people: three wannabe hunters and a self-serving idiot. My father would not have been pleased with me.*

***

A chunk of wood split open in the fiery flames and sent the fire blazing into the night sky. Jessica jumped, startled from her memories. She looked at each of her friends in turn before glancing at the moon. "Sorry, guys. It's getting late, and I think we should get some sleep."

"What about the rest of the story?" Rogue cried.

"It will have to wait for another time," Jessica said with a shake of her head. "Sleep first, story later."

"You can't leave us hanging like that," Imogen protested.

"I can, and I will. Go to bed, everyone," Jessica said. "We'll continue the story another time."

With much moping and grumbling, the group obeyed. As Jessica curled up next to Bear to sleep, she wondered what the next day would bring. As long as it wasn't more death, she'd be happy.

Chapter 5 - Lt. Cummings

Tomi left the Mayor's office and made straight for the supply depot. There was no time to waste. Not if they had to leave the following day. It was a pity. He'd hoped for some proper downtime. A good, long vacation with Marie, the kids, and the grandkids, but that wasn't meant to be. All thanks to the Mayor and her endless ambition. *Damn you, Maeve Finley.*

He encountered a young private at the depot and called the man over. "I need you to take a message to the following soldiers: Sergeant James Horton, Private Linda Longo, Private Sonja Barnes, Private Benjamin Plumm, Private Carl Thompson, Sergeant Irene O' Brian, and Private Lin Lee Chiang. These are their addresses."

The sergeant nodded as he jotted down the names and locations on a notepad, his expression earnest. "What is the message, Sir?"

"They are to report for duty at zero six hundred hours tomorrow morning," Lieutenant Cummings said.

"Yes, Sir," the private said.

"And if you hurry, there will be a recommendation in it for you," Tomi added. "The sooner my people know what's up, the sooner they can prepare."

"Yes, Sir!" the soldier said, ending off with a smart salute.

Tomi turned his attention to the next order of business: Securing supplies.

He booked two Humvees equipped with fifty caliber guns, spare tires, and several gallons of fuel. To that, he added food, water, first-aid kits, weapons, and ammunition, filling out the necessary paperwork and filing it with the clerk.

"Will that be all, Sir?"

"I need a car," Tomi said. "I'll return it in the morning."

"Of course, Sir. Just sign here," the clerk said, producing another set of papers.

Tomi heaved an inner sigh. Paperwork. The single thing he hated most in the world, yet it was everywhere.

"Here are your keys, Sir. It's the silver Ford sedan over there," the clerk added.

"Thank you," Tomi said, grabbing his duffle bag.

The car was a piece of shit. The door hinges were rusted, only one light worked, and the fan belt wailed like a banshee once he got it started. At least the heat worked. With a couple of bangs on the dashboard, hot air blasted from the vents, and he drove toward the gate with a smile on his face. *Ah, much better.*

"Have a good evening, Sir," the security guard at the exit said.

"Thank you, private," Lieutenants Cummings said with a brisk nod.

He drove through the city, navigating by the single headlight, and gazed around. The streets were quiet. Night had fallen, and the moon was nowhere to be seen, hidden behind a thick bank of clouds. The air smelled like rain, and he hoped the storm waited until he got to his destination.

It held off until the last minute. As Tomi drove up to his house, the clouds opened up and dumped a ton of water onto the earth below. Lightning flashed on the horizon, and thunder rumbled through the atmosphere. The wind picked up until it reached gale-force speeds, and he couldn't see a thing through the windshield.

Tomi drove at a snail's pace and crept up the road until he spotted the familiar red postbox that marked his driveway. He eased into the yard and parked underneath the carport. The flimsy structure shook with the onslaught of the storm, and one corner of iron sheeting flapped in the wind.

Lieutenant Cummings eyed the corrugated metal and swore. "Shit, I'll have to fix that before it —."

Even as he spoke, a gust of wind tore the sheet loose and whipped it into the night. Wide-eyed, Tomi stared into the dark. The storm was a lot worse than he'd thought, and it had only begun. *I'd better get my ass inside.*

He jumped out of the car and raced toward the porch, one hand clutching his duffel bag. Within moments, he was drenched to the bone and shivering. Taking the steps two at a time, he slammed a fist on the door. "Marie? Open up. It's me, Tomi."

Seconds later, the door opened to reveal the slender frame of his wife, Marie. She eyed him with a mixture of shock, surprise, and annoyance. "Tomi? Why didn't you warn me you were coming home?"

"I wanted it to be a surprise," Tomi yelled, struggling to be heard above the chaos all around them. Dead leaves swirled across the porch, whipped into a frenzy.

"Some surprise, showing up like a bedraggled alley cat in the middle of the night," Marie said with a sniff.

"I'm sorry, my love. Next time, I'll send a message," he said, trying to win her over. "Can I come in, please? It's raining something fierce out here, and it's piss cold."

"Of course it is," she said as if the weather was his fault as well.

Marie stepped aside to let him in and frowned. "You're not only late, but you're puddling all over my floor as well. What's next?"

Tomi gritted his teeth to refrain from snapping at her. It would be a mistake. The last thing he wanted was a fight with the missus on his only night off. "What a storm! It's like a hurricane out there."

"I hope not. That would be a real disaster."

"One of the metal sheets on the carport blew away," he continued, stamping his feet.

"I told you ages ago to fix that roof, but you never listen, and now it's too late," Marie scolded, heading toward the kitchen.

Tomi wanted to punch himself. He'd tried to distract her with talk of the storm. Instead, he'd reminded her of yet another one of his mistakes: Not fixing the carport roof. *Great. Just great.*

Marie returned moments later with a mop and chased him toward the bathroom. "Get out of those wet things and take a hot shower. I don't want you to get sick and die on me."

"You don't?" Tomi said with mock surprise.

Marie eyed him with displeasure, but the corner of her mouth twitched. Waving a hand, she said, "Off with you while I dry the floor and put the coffee pot on."

"Coffee sounds good," he said, further ingratiating himself before he hurried toward the bathroom.

Stripping off his wet clothes, Tomi stepped into a hot shower and washed the sweat and grime from his skin. The soap smelled like lemon, and he stepped out feeling refreshed and rejuvenated. Next, he dried off, wrapped the towel around his waist, and shaved.

He was almost done when Marie entered with a pile of clean clothes. "Here. I got you something to wear."

"Thank you," he said, eyeing her in the mirror.

To his relief, she smiled, her bad humor from before forgotten. "I'm glad you're home. I've missed you. It's not the same without you around."

"I missed you too, sweetheart," he said, leaning down to kiss her on the lips. A smear of shaving cream stayed behind, and he wiped it off with his thumb.

Marie took his hand in hers with a gentle smile. "You work too hard."

Tomi returned her smile, his heart growing warm inside his chest. This was what he longed for whenever he was away on a mission. "I do it for you."

"How long do I have you for this time?" Marie asked. "I'd like to invite the kids over for supper tomorrow. They'll be just as happy to see you as I am."

The smile slid off his face. "I can't stay for long. I only have tonight."

"You're kidding me!" Marie cried.

"The Mayor called me into her office and asked me to go on a critical assignment," Tomi said, rinsing the last bits of shaving cream from his face.

"I don't care who asked you. You're not going. This is ridiculous!" Marie said, slamming the bundle of clothes down on the floor. "One night!"

"I know, and I'm sorry, but I couldn't refuse," Tomi said.

"Couldn't refuse? Does she own you? Are you her slave?"

"No, but she is the mayor."

"I don't care who the hell she is. I won't allow it," Marie said, storming off.

Tomi quickly pulled on the clothes she'd left behind and ran after her. "Marie, please. If I do this, there's a big promotion in store for me."

Marie paused, her eyes narrowed. "Big promotion? How big?"

"Big enough that I won't have to take every job I'm offered. I can pick and choose, or I can send out other teams to do for me," Tomi said, spreading his hands wide.

Marie hesitated. "Really?"

Tomi nodded. "This is our chance, my love. A chance for me to spend more time with you and the kids."

"You promise? You're not lying to me?" she asked.

"Of course not. I'd never lie to you," Tomi said, taking her hands in his.

She gazed at him with those big blue eyes he loved more than anything in the world, and he held his breath. *Please say yes. I can't turn down this mission. I can't.*

Finally, she nodded. "Alright. You can go."

"Thanks. You won't regret this," Tomi said, blowing out a sigh of relief.

"We'll see about that, but enough for now. Let's get you settled in," Marie said, bustling toward the kitchen. "Hungry?"

"Starving."

"Supper is coming right up," Marie said.

He sat down at the table, and she handed him a cup of hot coffee followed by a plate of eggs, beans, fried ham, and biscuits. It smelled delicious and tasted even better. The food radiated heat throughout his body, and a sense of repletion flooded his senses. *I haven't felt this good in ages.*

Stifling a yawn, he leaned back in his chair and stretched out his legs. Marie tidied up the kitchen, humming her favorite tune beneath her breath while washing the dishes. The clinking of cups and saucers filled the air, the sound of home, while a fire crackled in the hearth. Outside, the storm raged unabated, but inside, it was a haven of peace and warmth.

Utterly relaxed, he allowed his thoughts to wander back to his conversation with Maeve Finley earlier. There was something off about her. Something wrong. He had the distinct feeling she'd do anything to get what she wanted, no matter the cost. The end justified the means in her mind.

Only, it didn't work that way in his. He'd experienced enough in his lifetime to know that it was always the innocent bystanders that got hurt, and in this case, it was the citizens of Vancouver who stood to lose the most through Maeve's machinations. The question was, what could he do about it? More importantly, should he do something about it?

Chapter 6 - Sandi

Sandi woke at the crack of dawn and stifled a gigantic yawn. Nestled against Paul's comforting warmth, she allowed herself to drift away on a languid tide of memories. They were visions of the past. Of a time when she and her friends looked forward to a bright future, young, strong, and vital. Afraid of nothing.

A time when Brittany was still alive, the Zoo was still their home, and half of the Exiles hadn't succumbed to the ravages of war and the Red Flux.

Still, as heavy as the weight of her sorrows were, Sandi did not regret the past. Brittany gave her life saving her friends, the Primes were free from the tyranny of Sikes and Douglas, the Red Flux was no more, they'd discovered another thriving colony of survivors, and they looked forward to rebuilding their home: The Zoo.

Moving with care, she slipped out of the bed and padded across the tiny room in her pajamas. She removed a thick jacket from the cupboard and shrugged it on, careful not to wake Paul. The poor man had spent a large chunk of the night on watch and needed to rest.

Cracking open the door, Sandi winced when a blast of cold air hit her in the face. Frost caressed her skin as she made her way across the deck, and she briefly considered going back.

With the jacket drawn tight around her chest, she gazed across the river. Her breath hitched in her throat, and she leaned against the railing, mesmerized.

The water shone like gold beneath the rays of the rising sun, and the banks were awash with tones of orange, yellow, and red. Streaks of mauve and lavender painted the clouds, and a flock of flyers crossed the far horizon.

The rhythmic chugging sound of the motor pushing them upstream toward the waiting docks came from the engine room. It was echoed by the bird calls, whoops, cries, and howls rising from the primordial forest that rose on either side. A dark and mysterious world filled with dangerous but wondrous creatures.

A smile tugged at Sandi's lips, and the deep-seated tension leached from her muscles. The sheer beauty of the world around her roused a sense of calm within her chest, and it felt as if a weight was lifted from her shoulders.

After the horrors of the past few months, she needed this reprieve. It was a chance to be young and carefree again. Unburdened by the cares and worries of Prime's infirmary and its ailing patients. No longer did she have to juggle a thousand-and-one responsibilities or stress about the coming day. *I can be me. Not Sandi the nurse, or Sandi the caregiver, or Sandi, Kat's second-in-command. Just me.*

A splash in the water caught her attention, and she bent over to get a better look. After a couple of seconds, the water rippled, and a long jagged fin broke the surface. It disappeared again, and she stared at the spot with deep concentration.

A monstrous head reared upward covered in thick silver scales that glinted in the light. Startled, Sandi jerked away, and her heart jumped into her throat. "What the hell is that?"

A glimpse of jagged teeth and a black eyeball was all she got before the fish slipped beneath the surface. Then another fin flashed past the boat, followed by another. The river churned, the water boiling as a school of vicious-looking fish swam past the boat.

Suddenly, a harpoon whistled past Sandi's shoulder. The steelhead buried itself deep within one of the creatures with a dull thunk. The fish thrashed, its blood staining the waters with a blossoming cloud of crimson. Then Ric was there, hauling on the line attached to the harpoon.

"Watch out," Ric cried, his teeth bared. He strained to pull in the fish, his muscles bulging beneath the material of his shirt. Sweat poured down his face, and he grunted with the effort of hauling in his catch.

Sandi danced to the side and out of his way. Caught utterly off-guard, she stared at the spectacle with wide eyes. "What are you doing?"

"What... do... you... think?" he asked between deep gasps for oxygen. "Catching... fish."

"What for?"

Ric flashed her a skeptical look. "Breakfast."

"Breakfast? You can't be serious," Sandi said, aghast. "That thing is a monster."

"Maybe, but it's good eating." He looked over his shoulder and yelled. "David? A little help here!"

"Coming," David cried, running toward them. He shot past Sandi, flashed her a grin, and jumped into the fray with both hands on the line.

Together, Ric and David fought with the fish for a solid twenty minutes before it grew tired. Its movements grew sluggish, the river running red with its life's blood. At last, it thumped against the side of the boat, and they wrestled it onboard.

The creature flopped around on the deck, its jaws lined with vicious-looking teeth. It snapped at anything within reach, and David nearly lost a finger when he got too close. Easily spanning three feet in length, it was a healthy specimen in its Prime.

Sandi watched from a healthy distance, both curious and afraid. In a way, she felt sorry for it, despite its ugly appearance. Like her, like any living being, it simply wanted to survive. Yet, here it was. Dying in the cold winter air to become food for a bunch of two-legged beasts.

She winced when Ric picked up a hammer and brained the fish with one mighty blow. It twitched a few more times, its tail fin flapping around before it sagged into death. Its inky black eyes grew dull, and it no longer seemed as fearsome.

"Poor thing," Sandi murmured.

"Poor thing? You must be joking," Ric said. "Poor me for going to all that trouble to catch one fish."

"It's not suffering anymore," David pointed out.

"True," Sandi admitted.

"Plus, it's a big one, and it should feed us all," Ric continued, removing the knife from his belt. He knelt next to his catch and gutted it with one smooth move, top to bottom. The innards spilled out onto the deck in a steaming pile of offal.

Sandi paled as the coppery tang of death coated her tongue. Her stomach revolted, and she barely made it to the railing in time. Convulsing, she vomited into the river, unable to stop herself.

"What on earth is wrong with you?" Ric asked.

"Sandi?" David asked.

Sandi didn't have an answer for either of them because she couldn't understand it herself. She wasn't squeamish, and she'd butchered many animals in her day. "I... I don't know."

"Are you alright, girl?" Ric asked with gruff concern.

"Do you need help?" David added.

Sandi wiped her mouth and shook her head. "No, I'm fine. I think I just need to lie down for a bit."

"Do that," Ric agreed. "I'll finish up here."

"Call me if you need anything," David said.

"Thank you, guys," Sandi said, stumbling past him toward her cabin. She crawled back into bed, tucking herself into Paul's warmth, and soon forgot about her delicate stomach.

Paul woke her up sometime after that, rolling over and kissing the tip of her nose. "Wake up, sleepyhead."

Sandi stirred and smiled. "Who are you calling a sleepy head? I was up long before you."

"I noticed," Paul said, drawing her into his arms.

"I watched the sunrise."

"And?"

"It was beautiful."

"Too bad I missed it."

"You missed the monster fish too."

"Monster fish?" Paul asked with one eyebrow raised.

Sandi told him about the school of fanged fish and Ric and David's struggles to catch one. She also told him about her sudden bout of illness.

"Are you okay now?" Paul asked, sitting upright.

"Much better. In fact, I feel great," Sandi said, leaping out of bed. "Let's get a move on."

"Now?" Paul said with a groan. "It's still early."

"So? You're missing out on all the scenery," Sandi said.

She danced around the room and pulled on her underwear, jeans, a t-shirt, socks, and trainers. The items were old and threadbare, remnants from Prime's stores. But they were clean and comfortable, and that was all that mattered to her.

She pulled her hair into a ponytail, brushed her teeth, and washed her hands and face with a bottle of water and a plastic bowl. While she finished her ablutions, she stared at the bowl. It was old and battered, its smooth surface scratched in places but otherwise intact even after all these years. *That thing is older than me.*

Sandi remembered distant conversations between the adults when she was younger. They often talked about plastic and the pollution it caused in the old world. Here, it was a blessing for nothing lasted except the once-controversial plastic. *Things sure have changed.*

That led her mind down a rabbit hole, and she looked at Paul with a quizzical frown. "Do you think they invented plastic in the future because they found some fossilized remains of it?"

"Huh?" Paul grunted.

"Then again, plastic things only came with us when the Shift happened. Without the Shift, it wouldn't be here," Sandi mused. "Or would it?"

"What?"

"What about our descendants? Do they change the future? Do we change the future?"

"You're making my head spin," Paul said with a groan.

"Or does everything stay the same because it was all supposed to happen like this?" she continued.

"Please, stop. It's much too early for riddles," Paul said.

"Never mind. I'm confusing the heck out of myself too," Sandi admitted.

Paul picked his shirt from the floor and sniffed it. "Still good."

"Yuck," Sandi said, pulling a face. "That's gross."

Paul ignored her comment and finished dressing. After washing up, they grabbed their jackets and headed outside.

The sun was up, the air crisp, and the sky blue. Birds called from the riverbanks, and a herd of Corythosaurus stood knee-deep in the water, feeding on weeds, tubers, and water-lilies. The placid dinos gazed at the boat as it chugged past, their duck-billed mouths and knobbed heads resembling their cousins, the Lambeosaurus.

Paul and Sandi stopped to admire the sight but were soon lured away by the smell of frying fish. They followed the scent and found David and Ric elbow-deep in flour. Fillets of battered fish sizzled in a deep pan next to them, and a basket of corn fritters steamed on the counter.

Ric's eyes lit up when he saw them, and he called, "You're just in time."

"What can we do?" Sandi asked.

"You can finish making the coffee," Ric said.

"And me?" Paul added.

"You can help me with the fish. I'm almost done."

"Happy to help," Paul said, removing his jacket and rolling up his sleeves.

While the men battered and fried the rest of the fillets, Sandi prepared a pot of strong coffee. The many delicious aromas formed a symphony of flavors, and her mouth watered. Gone was the strange fit of queasiness from that morning. She felt strong, healthy, and ready to start the day.

More than that. She was ready to face her parents, her friends, the Exiles, and most of all, Jamie. She hadn't seen or spoken to Brittany's mom since her friend's death, and she wasn't looking forward to it. At least, she wasn't alone. She had David and Paul for support. Together, they'd tell Jamie everything. Brittany died a hero, sacrificing her life for others, and her story deserved to be known.

Sandi had grown a lot and was no longer the naive young girl eager for adventure. The bloody hallways of Prime's infirmary had taught her much, and she no longer believed she was invincible. Paul and David too. They were ready, at last, to take up the mantle of responsibility their parents had tried to pass to them before. *It's time to put the past behind us and look to the future. A bigger, brighter future where we can all prosper, Primes and Exiles united side by side.*

Chapter 7

Rogue and the others packed up and hit the road before dawn the next day. They wanted to make up for lost time, and nobody wanted to linger in the area Spook died. With the boy dead and buried, they were eager to get moving, and by noon, they'd covered several miles. The terrain favored them, and they could stick to dry ground for the most part. Whenever they did hit water, it was shallow.

Rogue sat with her feet up on the dashboard, humming an old tune beneath her breath. Her mind roved far and wide, not focusing on their surroundings. Memories popped up at random, and she was soon lost in a fog of reverie.

"What's going on in that head of yours?" Seth asked, breaking the spell.

"Nothing much. Just remembering some stuff from the past."

"Like what?"

"Just stuff," Rogue said with a shrug. "Memories."

"Old boyfriends, perhaps?"

Rogue snorted. "There weren't many. Moran scared most of them away, and Bones took care of the rest."

Seth's expression darkened. "Bones."

"Yeah, I'd rather not talk about him," Rogue said with a shudder.

"What other secrets do you have?" Seth asked with a teasing grin.

"My life is an open book," Rogue said. "If you want to know something, just ask."

"Okay. What's your favorite color?" Seth asked.

"Really? Shouldn't you know that by now?"

"Err... Blue?" Seth guessed.

"Wrong. It's purple," Rogue said with a pout.

"Okay, okay. Tell me what happened to you the day of the Shift," Seth said. "You've told me a lot about your life on the streets of Prime, but never that. It's almost like you avoid it."

Rogue frowned. "That's because I don't like talking about it."

"Not even to me?"

"It's... complicated."

"Alright. Leave it then," Seth said, but she heard the edge in his voice.

"Fine. I'll tell you, but only if you tell me how you got that scar on your face," Rogue countered.

"I told you already. I fought with a guard from the Watch," Seth said.

"So you say, but I never got the whole story," Rogue said.

Seth looked at her but didn't reply.

"It's only fair. A story for a story," Rogue said, tapping her feet on the dashboard.

Seth sighed. "Okay. It's a deal."

"Excellent," Rogue said with a grin. "I'll start."

She drew a deep breath and told him everything, starting at the beginning. It was a long story. Some of it, he already knew, but she repeated it anyway. It passed the time and took her mind off her surroundings. Though some of what she relayed was traumatic, the memories were old and lacked any real sting.

"My mom dropped me off at school that morning, and I had no idea what would happen that day. None of us did. Suddenly, the classroom shook, and this strange shimmer appeared out of nowhere. It looked almost… pretty. I wanted to touch it, but something told me not to. The teacher and the rest of the kids were on the other side. She called me, but it was too late. The next minute they were gone, and I was here. Alone."

As Rogue spoke, her mind flew back in time, and she remembered in vivid detail what it was like that day. The nauseating jump in time that left her feeling off-balance and shaky. The sudden disappearance of the teacher and her classmates. And in its place, the primordial world with all of its hidden dangers, secrets, and seductive beauty.

Trees as tall as skyscrapers rose all around, making her feel small and inconsequential. Vines as thick as her waist hung from the branches, and the ground was covered in emerald green moss. Exotic flowers the color of blood blossomed on a nearby bush, and another one hung heavy with yellow berries. They looked delicious and also dangerous.

"I almost got squashed when a herd of Ankylosaurusus stampeded past the classroom. I hid under one of the desks and stayed there until a kind couple rescued me. Mike and Corinne. They took me with them to Prime Hotel looking for answers and refuge."

"Did you find it?" Seth asked.

Rogue shrugged. "In a way, I suppose. We learned about the Shift, though I could never understand how the scientists that caused it could be so careless."

"They suffered from a God complex and thought they could do anything they wanted," Seth said.

Rogue nodded. "And look where that got us. Families torn apart, thousands of people stranded in a hostile environment. Forever."

"What happened to Mike and Corinne?" Seth asked. "You never told me much about them."

Rogue hesitated. "Mike sacrificed himself for me. For us. He was a brave man and a real hero." Once more, she was swept away on a tide of memories and sensations until it felt like she was there.

***

They struck out into the busy street, and the chaos enveloped them. They fought their way through the crowds, drawing ever closer to their destination. Lillian soon grew tired, but she didn't dare complain. Nobody else did. Instead, she forced her legs to keep moving.

"Come on, sweetie," Corinne said. "We're almost there."

Suddenly, screams broke out, and people scattered in all directions. Lillian grabbed Corinne's leg. "What's happening?"

Corinne never got the chance to answer as a giant monster charged toward them. Its colossal head dipped in and out of the crowd, snapping at anything that moved. Blood sprayed into the air, and the screaming grew frantic. Its hind legs were the size of tree trunks, and they bowled over everything without pause.

Mike hustled them into the nearest shop. "Over there. Get inside!"

They'd almost made it when someone bumped into Lillian. She lost her hold on Corinne and whirled about in fright. An elbow hit her in the head, and she fell to the ground with a cry. On her hands and knees, she scrambled toward a nearby wall and pressed her back against it. "Corinne! Mike!"

The Tyrannosaurus rex charged down the sidewalk, one clawed foot crushing the hood of a parked car. It paused when it spotted

Lillian, and its beady eyes fixed on her shaking form. It stepped closer, each movement sending a mass of vibrations through the concrete.

Lillian stared at the approaching nightmare and kept screaming. It was all she could do. Scream, and scream, and cry. She had no weapons and no super strength. She wasn't a comic book hero or a soldier. She was a nobody.

The T-Rex lowered its head toward her. Its lips peeled back to reveal teeth the length of her forearms. Rancid breath washed across her face, and she knew it was going to eat her.

Suddenly, Mike was there. He grabbed her by the scruff of her neck and tossed her aside. She tumbled across the concrete and lay watching helplessly.

As the T-Rex closed in for the kill, Mike jammed his gun into its mouth and pulled the trigger. Bullets punched into the monster's open maw, shattering bone and flesh. Blood poured from the creature's ruptured cranium and misted the air.

The T-Rex reared back with a shriek of agony before it reacted in pure rage. It snapped at Mike, and its teeth closed over his torso. The dinosaur shook the man back and forth like a rag doll, the crackle of his ribs and spine loud in Lillian's ears.

She reached out a hand in despair. "Mike, no!"

Next to her, Kat and Corinne cried out with equal horror. Yet, they could do nothing but watch as the scene unfolded.

With a rattling roar, the T-Rex dropped Mike's mangled form and collapsed to the ground with a thunderous crash. It twitched a couple of times before it grew still. Dead, at last.

Kat sprinted toward her uncle's body, cradling his broken form to her chest. "No! You can't die, Uncle. You're all I have left."

But Mike was gone, his final breath leaving his lungs in a rush of blood. Corinne gathered the crying Lillian into her arms before shouting to Kat. "We need to go. We need to get to the hotel."

Kat shook her head, her expression fierce. "No! I'm not leaving him."

"It's what he would've wanted, Kat. Please," Corinne pleaded. "We need to get to safety."

Kat's shoulders shook as she lowered Mike's body to the ground. She grabbed his gun and dashed away her tears. "Fine. Let's go."

"Come on, Lillian. We need to run," Corinne said.

"No, I want to see Mike," Lillian said, shaking her head.

"Mike is dead, sweetie, and we need to leave now." Corinne hauled Lillian to her feet and dragged her by the arm.

At first, Lillian fought against her hold. She didn't want to run, didn't want to go anywhere. She wanted to go back to Mike and tell him she was sorry. But Corinne was relentless, and Lillian had no option to obey.

Twenty minutes later, they stumbled through the gates of the Prime Hotel. High walls surrounded it, and the vast grounds bustled with activity. Excavators, trucks, and loaders rumbled about while men wearing hard hats swarmed the building site. The hotel itself was still a shell, but transport trucks filled with furniture and other supplies kept arriving in a steady stream.

Armed police officers waved them to a field of tents set up in one of the clearings. Ambulances were parked in front of a field hospital, and wounded people were rushed inside stretchers.

A woman with a clipboard rushed toward them and took down their names, ages, and occupation. While Corinne did her best to answer, Lillian stared at the flood of desperate refugees streaming toward the gate.

They were pushed aside when a vintage Bentley roared through the gates. The man inside paused to shout an order to the armed police before racing toward the hotel. Seconds later, the police formed *a wall of firepower in front of the entrance.*

The people streaming toward the hotel were turned away by the threatening barrels of loaded guns. One policeman picked up a loudspeaker and announced, "Citizens of Portland. The grounds are full. We've reached maximum capacity. Please, leave in an orderly fashion. Head to your homes or the nearest community center."

The crowd roared with protest, jamming their fists in the air. Mothers with children pressed to the front, pleading with the police to take their babies. The policeman with the speaker shook his head. "Leave now, or we will be forced to open fire."

"What are they doing?" Corinne asked the woman with the clipboard. "Surely, they have to let those people in. They'll die out there."

"I'm afraid it's Mr. Douglas' decision. He's the owner of this hotel, and we're full up," the woman replied with a cold expression. "You can be glad you made it in time. As it is, you'll have to work to earn your keep. This is not a charity organization."

"But...that's wrong!"

"That's the way it is, Mrs. Marshall. If you don't like it, you and your children can leave."

"She's not my mother," Kat said in an expressionless voice.

"Either way. You can go if you want. Now's your chance," the woman said before moving toward the next bundle of people waiting in line.

Corinne shook her head, one hand pressed to her lips. "We can't leave. It's not safe out there."

"No, it's not," Kat said. "For better or worse, we're here now, and we have to stay."

Lillian listened to it all with growing confusion. Meantime, the crowd at the gate was gathering momentum. Their anger grew palpable, and several men stormed the entrance.

Without hesitation, the police opened fire on the crowd. A hot stream of lead cut through the refugees, and several people collapsed to the ground with screams of pain—women, children, and men alike. The rest streamed away from the hotel in a panic. Soon, the field in front of the hotel was empty but for the corpses of those who'd died.

With a horrified cry, Corinne hustled Lillian and Kat away from the sight. She was too late, though. They could never unsee what they'd seen, and the guilt of that moment would haunt them forever.

***

"I remember that day," Seth said. "I made it through the gates in the nick of time. That was the day Prime was born, and the Exiles became its enemies."

"It was appalling," Rogue said, her ears still ringing with the echoes of gunshots and screams.

"What about Corinne?" Seth asked.

"She tried her best to look after us girls, but it was an impossible task. There was never enough food to go around, and she worked herself to the bone. Eventually, she became so weak she contracted pneumonia. It didn't take long for her to die." Rogue dashed away a tear

"It must've been hard for you," Seth said. "You were only five."

"No harder than it was for anybody else," Rogue said.

"What about Kat?"

"She had her own demons to fight," Rogue said. "Just like I did."

"That was some story," Seth said.

"Yup, and now it's your turn," Rogue said, turning toward him.

"Okay, but I'm warning you. It's a long story."

"I'm all ears." Rogue settled back in her seat with a packet of trail mix in her lap and a grin on her face. She loved stories, and this was going to be a good one. She just knew it.

Chapter 8 - Seth

Seth smoothed the brush over the mule's coat, removing the dirt and sweat accumulated after a long day's work in the fields. The animal stamped a lazy hoof, and its tail flicked at the annoying insects that sought to feed on its rich blood.

"That's a good boy," Seth said, patting the animal on the rump. The mule rolled its eyes at him and blew a cloud of warm air from its nostrils. "Yeah, yeah, I'm done. Off to bed with you."

He led the animal to its stall and ensured there was a pail of fresh water and a flake of hay for the tired mule. Afterward, he toured the stables and checked that all the animals were in for the night, fed, watered, and groomed. They were his responsibility, and their wellbeing was his highest priority. One by one, he checked the stalls until he reached the last one. It was empty. "What the hell?"

Seth frowned, and the beginnings of anger stirred within his breast. Jelly was missing, and he had a feeling it didn't bode well for the young donkey. Her newest handler was a former member of the Watch and the nephew of Senator Douglas. Unable to hack it as a soldier, he'd been assigned as an overseer of the fields instead.

Thus far, he'd created nothing but problems for all involved, especially Seth. Lazy and shiftless, the man possessed a cruel streak, and Seth harbored the suspicion that he abused the animals when no one was looking. Despite this belief, his hands were tied. Maybury outranked him, and he dared not confront the man or risk losing his job.

Seth headed toward the fields but didn't have far to go. Within seconds, he heard the frantic braying of a donkey in severe distress, followed by the crack of a whip. He rounded the corner of a storage building and spotted Maybury and Jelly.

The overseer lashed the animal with an expression of glee on his face. He grunted with the effort of each blow, intent on inflicting the maximum amount of pain and suffering. Tied to a post, the helpless Jelly bucked and kicked to no avail. Foam flecked her mouth, and saliva drooled onto her chest in long silver strings. Her eyes rolled in their sockets, and blood shone on her flanks.

Rage infused Seth's mind, and all rational thought fled instantly. With a cry of fury, he barreled toward Maybury with his fists clenched and raised to strike. "You asshole!"

Maybury stopped mid-blow, and his eyes widened with shock. He stumbled back a few steps and raised one hand in the air. "Hey, now hold on."

Seth ignored him, committed to the act. He lashed out and landed a solid blow on Maybury's jaw. The man went flying and rolled across the packed earth in a cloud of dust. He coughed and shook his head, a trickle of crimson flowing from a split lip.

"Don't you dare lay a hand on these animals. We need them, you idiot," Seth said through gritted teeth.

Within seconds, Maybury was back on his feet, his face engorged with fury. "Who do you think you are? I can do whatever the hell I want."

"Oh, yeah? Try it, asshole," Seth said, flexing his shoulders.

Maybury raised the whip and swung at Seth. It cracked with a sound akin to lightning, too fast for the naked eye to follow.

Seth tried to duck, but he was too late. The leather tip cut into his flesh, splitting the skin across his face. Fiery agony raced through his nerve-endings, and he cried out with shock. Hot blood poured from the wound and dripped onto his shirt. His eye swelled shut in an instant, and he was left off-balance.

Maybury took his chance and ran toward Seth. His fist connected with a thud, and Seth's head snapped to the side. Blood filled his mouth, and he spat it out with a grimace. He ducked beneath a second blow and danced out of reach while he collected his wits. "Try that again, Maybury. I dare you."

With a furious roar, Maybury launched himself forward. But this time, Seth was ready for him. He connected with a right hook that caused Maybury to grunt with surprise and followed up with a jab to the face and another hit to the stomach.

Maybury stumbled back, shaking his head, but Seth didn't let up for one second. He rained down a barrage of blows and finished off by ramming his shoulder into the man's stomach.

Seth stepped back as Maybury went down like a sack of potatoes. Breathing hard, he watched as the man rolled around on the ground, groaning with pain. Both his eyes were swollen shut, his nose broken, and his lips smashed to a pulp. He wasn't getting up soon. "Have you had enough, Maybury?"

"Damn you, Seth. I'll make sure you pay for this," Maybury mumbled.

And pay Seth did. Within hours, he was locked up and charged with attempted murder. Still, he made sure that Maybury was removed from his post first and could no longer torment the animals. Even his uncle, Senator Douglas, wasn't about to risk the lives of the city's remaining livestock. Without them, Prime City was doomed. Just like Seth.

As he sat shivering in the dungeons, Seth contemplated his fate. It would come down to a simple choice: A single bullet to the head or banishment. Both meant death, but the latter held the promise of freedom.

Most people would disagree with that choice. They'd see banishment as a horrific punishment. Exiled from the safety of the city's walls, one would be left to wander the harsh Primordial world filled with ferocious predators: T-rexes, raptors, and a myriad of other creatures.

Still, Seth believed he stood a chance. He'd spent the early part of his life in Alaska, hunting, foraging, trapping, and navigating the wilds at his father's side. Granted, it was a different world, but he was sure he could do it again. *I have to keep my wits about me.*

With his decision made, he tried to sleep, for who knew what awaited him on the other side of the wall? He'd need all of his strength if he wanted to survive, and he'd be damned if he failed.

***

"There you have it," Seth said with a shrug. "The story of how I got kicked out of Prime."

"That was quite a story. I'm glad you told me," Rogue said, eating the last of her trail mix. She wiped her hands on her jeans and gazed ahead. "And it made the hours go by much faster. The day is almost over."

"Almost," Seth agreed, glancing at the sun. It hung low on the horizon, a sure sign they'd set up camp soon.

He steered the truck around a clump of brush, careful to stick to the path made by the vehicles ahead. He and Rogue were the last in line, with Ronan in the lead. It was probably the safest position for them as any mishaps in terrain would hit the lead truck first.

Until…

The narrow muddy track dipped down into a patch of water, and Seth saw it an instant too late. He hit the water at full speed, and brown sludge splashed all over the nose and windshield.

"What the hell?" Rogue yelled and quickly closed her window, but it was too late. They were both sopping wet and covered in filth.

"Sorry," Seth said, gritting his teeth.

"Yuck, I'm soaked in bog juice," Rogue said, wrinkling her nose.

Seth squinted at the windscreen, but it was covered with a layer of the same stuff they were stewing in. He switched on the wipers, but they were old and cracked. Instead of clearing the crap away, it smeared it all over the glass.

Unable to see the way ahead, Seth veered off course. When he realized they were on the wrong path, he slammed on the brakes, and they slid to a muddy stop a few feet away.

"Seth?" Rogue yelled again, her face turning purple. "What are you doing?"

"I said, I'm sorry," Seth said, reaching for the radio.

"Just get us out of here," Rogue said with a huff.

"Jessica, are you there? Over," Seth said into the radio.

"Go ahead. Over," came the quick reply.

"We had a little accident. Over."

"Do you need help? Over."

"Not really. I have to clean the windshield and get back on track. Give us a few minutes to catch up. Over."

"Got it. I'll inform the rest, and we'll wait for you. Over,"

Jessica said.

"Thanks. Over and out."

Seth replaced the radio and removed an old rag from the cubby hole. "Sit tight, babe. I'll be right back."

"Um, Seth," Rogue said in a small voice.

"Yes?" Seth asked, pausing for a moment.

"Why is there mud oozing into the cab?"

"What?" Seth cried, looking down at the spot she pointed. Sure enough. Blackish-grey sludge crept in through the gap under the door. "It's probably just a splash."

Together, they watched as more and more of the stuff filled the footwell. When it began to come in through the pedals as well, Rogue shook her head. "That's more than just a splash."

"Okay. Stay calm. Don't panic," Seth said.

Rogue didn't listen. Instead, she grabbed the door handle and turned.

"No!" Seth yelled, but he needn't have bothered.

Nothing happened.

"It won't open. Why won't it open?" Rogue cried.

That was when Seth realized the truth. "It won't open because the mud is pressing against the doors from the outside."

"What does that mean?" Rogue asked with wide eyes.

"It means we're a lot deeper into the stuff than I thought," Seth said. *Maybe even too deep to get out.*

Chapter 9

Rogue yanked on the door handle with all her might. When it wouldn't budge, she threw her body against it until her shoulder was bruised and swollen. A sob crept up her throat, but she swallowed it with an effort. "Come on, come on, please!"

"Stop it. It won't work," Seth said, placing one hand on her arm.

Rogue was tempted to ignore him, but he was very insistent. That and the fact that she needed someone to rely on. She needed someone to be strong for her because this was her worst nightmare come true. "I can't do this, Seth. I can't be trapped. I just can't."

"Shh, sweetheart. It's okay," Seth said, pulling her into his arms. With one hand, he smoothed her hair while holding her close. "You're not trapped. We're just stuck in a bit of mud."

"You call that a bit?" she asked, pointing at the ooze in the footwell. It moved higher and higher until she pulled her feet up onto the seat. "Do something!"

"Hold on," Seth said, pulling away.

Feeling bereft, she reached for him, but he had already opened the window and leaned out. "What do you see?"

"It's about a third of the way up," he replied, dropping back into his seat.

"Let me see," Rogue said, opening her window.

"Rogue, don't. It will only upset you," Seth said.

She waved him away. "Radio for help, why don't you?"

"I was about to do that," Seth said.

He picked up the mic and called to Jessica. "Come in, please. Jessica, come in. Over."

"Go ahead, Seth."

"We need assistance. I repeat. We need assistance," Seth said. "We are stuck in the mud, and we can't get out on our own. Over."

"Got it. We are on our way. Sit tight," Jessica said. "Over."

"Thanks. Over and out," Seth said. "You hear that? They are on their way."

"That's wonderful news, except for one thing," Rogue said.

"What's that?"

"We're sinking."

"What?" Seth cried, turning pale.

"You heard me. We're sinking," Rogue repeated.

Seth leaned out the window again, staring down. After a few seconds, he nodded. "You're right. We are sinking. We must've landed in a pool of quicksand."

"Quicksand?" Rogue said, her voice shrill. "We landed in quicksand?"

"Don't worry. Everything will be alright, I promise," Seth said.

"How would you know? The truck is sinking into a pit of liquid sand, and we're sitting inside it. Nothing about this is alright!" Rogue said.

"Rogue, please. Calm down," Seth pleaded.

"I can't calm down. It's halfway up the door now."

"Let's take a moment to think. There has to be a way out of this," Seth said.

"Try driving out," Rogue suggested.

Seth leaned out the window again and looked around. When he dropped back in, he shook his head. "I wouldn't know which way to go. We're surrounded, and I might just drive us in deeper. Besides, I doubt we'd be able to move at all. The stuff is like glue."

"Damn it!" Rogue slammed both hands against the door and screamed. Rational thought gave way to panic, and she couldn't control the fear that coursed through her veins. She hated being confined in small spaces and dreaded the thought of drowning or smothering. "I have to get out. I can't be stuck in here. I can't."

"Rogue!" Seth grabbed her arm. "You mustn't panic."

"Leave me alone. We'll die in here. Look," she insisted, pointing at the mud in the footwell. It had reached the edge of the seat and threatened to leak over. "We have to get out while we still can."

"Alright," Seth said. "Grab your stuff and get onto the roof. It will buy us some time, at least."

"Thank God," Rogue said, reaching for her bag and rifle. She slung both onto her back before she crawled out of the window. The bog bubbled below, beckoning with its promise of a slow, horrifying death.

Looking away, she twisted around and gripped the edge of the roof. Inch by inch, she pulled herself upward and clambered on top of the trunk. With a sigh of relief, she slumped to her knees.

"Seth, are you coming out or not?" she called.

"Almost there," he said with a grunt, joining her moments

later.

They huddled together and looked around, alarmed to find themselves surrounded by a sea of muddy ooze. It all looked the same, and all or none of it could be quicksand.

"Now what?" Rogue asked.

"Now we wait for the others," he said, pulling her close.

It didn't take long for the rest of the group to show up. They hadn't been very far ahead to begin with. Circling the worst of the bog, they parked and got out to study the situation.

"Are you okay?" Imogen called, her expression pinched.

"Never better," Rogue replied, feeling testy.

Ronan whistled. "Quite a pickle you've got yourself in. I'm impressed."

"Oh, shut up, Ronan," Jessica said, waving him off. "We have to get them out of there."

"The truck's a goner," Nigel said. "We'll never get it out."

"That's true," Ronan said. "Any ideas?"

"It's simple," Nigel said with a shrug. "We find the shallowest side, throw down a carpet of leaves and branches, and they jump. With any luck, they can crawl to dry land."

"And if we can't? If we sink?" Rogue asked, aghast.

"Then we throw you a rope and pull you out," Nigel added.

"Wonderful plan," Rogue said, shaking her head.

"Do you have a better idea?" Nigel asked. He looked around. "Do any of you?"

Silence met his question.

"No? Then I guess we'd better get to work," Nigel said.

Removing the machete from his belt, he headed toward the nearest clump of bushes and hacked off an armful of branches. The others caught on and pitched in to help, collecting a huge pile of vegetation.

While they were busy, Ronan picked up a long stick and tested the ground. "Over here, guys. This seems to be the closest we can get."

Meanwhile, Rogue and Seth sat on the roof of the sinking truck, watching the mud come closer and closer. It was almost as if they were waiting to die, their very existence a throw of the dice. Would Nigel's plan work? Or wouldn't it?

"I can't stand this," Rogue said. Her gaze was fixed on the bog below, watching as the greedy earth swallowed them whole. With every passing second, they sank deeper into the ground.

"I know, but it's just a little longer," Seth said, squeezing her hand.

"Is it?" Rogue muttered, wondering what lay below the surface below. How many other unfortunate creatures had stumbled into the pit of liquid death? How many corpses lay rotting in the deep. Forgotten.

Preoccupied with her morbid thoughts, she paid little attention to the group and their efforts. Instead, she clung to Seth for comfort and measured the hours of her life in inches of mud. *Is this the way it ends?*

"Alright. Your magic carpet awaits," Ronan called, releasing her from the fog.

"What?"

"Your magic... you know what? Forget it. Just get your ass over here before it's too late," Ronan said with more than a hint of annoyance. "We've lost too much time already."

Something in his tone set her off, and Rogue jumped to her feet. "Well, I'm ever so sorry for the inconvenience, asshole. Let me not delay you any further."

With those words, she launched herself from the truck's roof, pushing off as hard as she could. For a brief moment, she was airborne, suspended above the earth. It was a strange sensation, and she felt as free as a bird.

The feeling didn't last. Like all good things, it came to an abrupt end. The ground rushed up, and she belly-flopped into the mud with all the grace and finesse of a blue whale. The air left her lungs with a whoosh, and pain shot through her rib cage. It radiated outward and left her gasping like a fish out of water.

"Rogue, are you alright?" Seth called. "Answer me, please."

"Ugh. I'm fine," she managed to say, each word sending a spike through her brain. "Did I make it?"

"It looks like it," Nigel said. "You're not sinking."

"That's good to know," Rogue said, blinking the tears from her eyes. She crawled forward on her hands and knees until people reached out to help her to her feet.

Nigel attempted to dust her off but gave up with a grimace of disgust. "You stink."

"Thanks," Rogue said, quirking her brows.

He handed her a handkerchief. "It's my last one. Wipe your face."

Rogue did as he suggested, removing the gunk from her cheeks. While she was busy, Seth followed her example and jumped. He was a lot better at it, landing on his feet like a real champion.

"Are you okay?" he asked again, rushing to her side.

"I'm fine."

"Your truck isn't," Nigel said.

Rogue turned to watch in time to see the vehicle sink below the sea of mud, a couple of air bubbles its last hurrah. She swallowed hard, cold fear forming a knot in her stomach. *We were lucky this time. But for how much longer?*

Chapter 10 - Lt. Cummings

The Humvee rattled across the broken track, and Lieutenant Cummings clung to the window frame with one hand and the dashboard with the other. It didn't help much. His body swayed from side to side, and he had to clamp his jaws shut to prevent himself from biting his tongue to shreds. When the front tire hit a rock, he became airborne for a few nerve-wracking seconds before slamming back down in his seat. "Holy shit, Sergeant. Are you trying to kill me?"

"Trying, Lieutenant? Of course not. Want to? Maybe," James quipped with a crooked grin.

"I feel like a martini. Shaken, not stirred," Tomi griped.

"A martini would've been nice right about now," Private Linda Longo said, flashing him a mean look.

Tomi rolled his eyes but refrained from answering. None of the crew were particularly happy with him for dragging them on another assignment so soon. Not that he had a choice. It was that or suffer Maeve Finley's wrath. Something he'd rather not incur without some sort of backup. *They'll understand soon enough. If everything works out according to plan, this trip will mean a better future for all of us.*

He turned his attention to Sonja up in the turret. "See anything, Private Barnes?"

"Nothing, Sir. But visibility is poor," she replied.

"Honestly, I can't see shit either," James said.

"Damn it," Tomi said, squinting at their surroundings.

The trees rose on either side of the narrow game trail, and thick vines hung from the branches like green streamers. A layer of damp moss and rotting leaves created a slippery carpet underneath the wheels, and James had a tough time keeping the truck on the straight and narrow.

Even worse, the canopy blocked most of the sunlight, reducing their visibility to almost zero. They could only see a few yards ahead which created a dangerous situation. One that played havoc with his nerves. A game trail equaled game, which meant trouble in anyone's book. *I knew we should've gone around.*

But going around meant adding two days to the journey, and he had no time to waste. Rogue and the rest of her group would've reached the inland sea by now. After that, it was three or four days tops before they arrived at the research facility, and he meant to be there when they did. That meant taking a shortcut through the middle of the primordial forest instead of sticking to the open like Rogue's party had done.

They'd tracked the Primes from Vancouver to the house where they'd spent the night. Tomi surmised the building belonged to either Ronan or Jessica, a haven in the wilderness. It was clever, and his estimation of them rose a notch.

From the house, he'd followed them north until they reached the belt of trees. Rogue and the rest had gone around while he elected to cut through it. He was playing a dangerous game, and he knew it. Then again, they had the fifty-calibers, a powerful deterrent to any creature they faced. *We can do this. We have to.*

They continued on their journey, and the hours passed

excruciatingly slowly. Each minute added another bruise to his already battered frame, and Tomi doubted he'd ever be the same again.

Suddenly, the trees began to thin, and the narrow track expanded into a rough open field. Hope rose within his chest, and Lieutenant Tomi leaned forward in his chair to look ahead. "Are we through the forest?"

"Yes, we are, Sir," James said, but his voice was subdued.

"What is it? What's wrong?" Tomi asked.

"We're through the trees, but look at that," James said, pointing ahead.

Tomi squinted through the windshield, and the saliva in his mouth dried up. He swallowed on the knot in his throat, but it refused to budge.

In front of them was an open field stretching as far as the eye could see. The knee-high stalks undulated in the breeze like a golden sea, the perfect grazing ground for a herd of dinosaurs. They dotted the plain in vast numbers, a mixed bag of herbivores: Triceratops, Lambeosaurus, Alamosaurus, Achelousaurus, Parksosaurus, and Ankylosaurus, to name but a few.

"That field is trouble," Linda said with a brisk shake of the head.

"We can't go through that. It's impossible," Sonja said.

"What do we do now, Sir?" James asked.

Tomi hesitated, but he knew there was no choice. Going back or around would cost them too much time. Days of travel that they simply didn't have. Not if they wanted to complete their mission and catch up with the Primes and their partners. He needed that research. Needed it for reasons of his own.

A glance at his watch revealed it was a little past noon. "Let's take a break."

James nodded and parked the Humvee. He reached for the radio and held the mic to his lips. "Thompson? Private Thompson, you there? Over."

"I'm here, Sergeant. Over," Thompson, the driver of the second Humvee, responded.

"We're taking a break. Over," James said.

"Copy that, Sergeant. Over," Thompson said.

"Over and out," James said, replacing the mic.

The two Humvees stopped next to each other, and the doors opened. Team members poured out onto packed earth and bustled around the vehicle. Plumm headed straight for the food supplies and handed out snacks and water. O' Brian lit a cigarette, a rare commodity in the city. Expensive too. The coal burned brightly against her pale, freckled skin, the same color as her orange hair. The rest milled about. Some took bathroom breaks while others stretched their legs.

Lieutenant Cummings walked the perimeter and studied the herd. They were calm for the moment, grazing in the rich fodder without a hint of alarm. Placid and peaceful. Not even the presence of the two vehicles and their occupants seemed to faze them.

With a pair of binoculars, Tomi studied the edges of the field. If there were carnivores lurking about, that was where they'd be.

"See anything?" James asked, joining him.

"Nothing out of the ordinary."

"Okay," James said, sitting down on a wooden stump. He took a swig of water from a canteen and offered the rest to Tomi.

"No, thank you," Tomi said, waving him off. "I'm not thirsty, just impatient."

"Me too," James said. "I didn't get to spend much time at home this last run."

"It couldn't be helped," Tomi said, unapologetic.

"Uh-huh," James said, eyeing him from underneath his lashes. "You haven't told us much about this mission. Only that we have to retrieve something and rescue the mayor's daughter."

"It's classified," Tomi said.

"I see," James said, his expression thoughtful. "I just hope it's worth it."

"It is. Have I ever let you down," Tomi asked. "Trust me."

"Alright. You've always steered us right in the past," James said with a shrug.

Tomi grunted, unwilling to say anything further about the mission. Instead, he added, "Be careful. That's all I can say. Be careful and watch your back."

"Yes, Sir. I'll do that," James acknowledged, getting back to his feet.

Sergeant Irene O' Brian sauntered toward them, a smoke dangling from her fingers. "How do ye propose we get across that field, Lieutenant?"

"Through there," Lieutenant Cummings said, handing her the binoculars. "The herd is at its thinnest there, plus it's mostly Lambeosaur's and Parksosaurus'. They're known to be placid. If we go slow and stay away from them, we can make it without spooking the lot."

Irene nodded. "Tis a solid plan."

"Let me see," James said, reaching for the binoculars. He studied the spot then pointed to the side. "What about that low rocky ridge? We can use it as a shield."

Tomi and Irene took turns examining the ridge.

"'Tis brilliant," Irene cried, punching James on the shoulder.

"Err, thanks," he said, rubbing the bruised flesh.

Tomi grinned. He liked Irene for what she was: Uncomplicated, honest, and without airs. With her, it was a case of what you see is what you get.

With their strategy decided, he gave the order. "Let's move. Break time's over."

Within seconds, the Humvees were loaded and ready to go. Sonja and Chiang occupied their posts at the fifty calibers, prepared to fire should things go wrong while James and Carl took the drivers' seats. Irene and Tomi each had a pair of binoculars and would serve as navigators.

"Remember, slow and steady wins the race. Don't panic, and don't shoot at anything unless it's absolutely necessary," Lieutenant Cummings said over the radio. "Over."

"'Tis no bother, Lieutenant. It'll be fine," Irene said with supreme confidence.

James was not so sure. "Are we really going through that?"

"Yes, we are," Tomi said, determined. "Let's go."

"Yes, Sir," James said, turning the key in the ignition. He drove toward the herd at a slow but steady pace, both hands on the wheel.

Tomi watched the herd through his binoculars, ready to give directions. As they drew closer, a sense of foreboding filled him. Was he doing the right thing? Or was he risking all of their lives for nothing? *I guess we'll find out soon enough.*

Chapter 11 - Sandi

After a superb breakfast of battered fish, corn fritters, and coffee, Sandi whiled away the rest of the morning on the deck. She sat on a wooden bench, with a pile of clothes at her feet. The garments needed mending, and she happened to be an expert seamstress.

Her needle flashed in the sun as she bent to her task, a tuneless song on her lips. With dainty stitches, she sewed together the ragged seam and tied off the thread in a knot. Holding the shirt up to the light, she smiled with satisfaction. "There you go. You can hardly see the tear."

Sandi folded up the shirt, set it aside, and dragged a pair of jeans onto her lap. Her needle flashed again as she got to work, her brow furrowed with concentration. The hours passed quickly, occupied as she was with her task. Before long, they bumped up against the jetty, and the boat's motor stopped running.

"Are we here?" Sandi asked, looking around.

"Yes, we are," Paul said. "Let's pack our things."

Sandi gathered up her sewing kit and the rest of the clothes before making her way to the cabin. Along the way she encountered David and handed him a pair of jeans, socks, and gloves. "Here you go. I fixed them for you."

"Thanks a million, Sandi," David said with a brilliant smile.

"My pleasure." She continued onward and returned the Captain's jacket, as well, followed by a couple of deck hand's shirts, and Ric's favorite hat. They all thanked her with beaming smiles and much bowing and scraping.

"Thank you, kindly, young miss. May fortune smile upon you and yours," the Captain said, his speech even more flowery than usual.

"Bless you, girl. I thought it was a goner, for sure," Ric said, jamming the hat onto his head like a squashed mushroom.

By the time she reached her cabin, Sandi felt like the Queen of the Nile, albeit an out-of-breath one.

"Where have you been?" Paul asked.

"Deliveries," Sandi said, pulling a face at him.

He stared at her for a second then shrugged. "Whatever. I've packed most of our stuff. Let's go."

Sandi followed him outside, her bag slung across her back and was met with a scene of ordered chaos.

"Look alive, folks. Secure the boat, and get ready to unload!" the Captain ordered and several deckhands scrambled to tie the boat to the jetty.

Afterward, they emptied the cargo hold, laid down a gangplank, and carried an assortment of boxes, crates, weapons, and other supplies onto the banks. That was loaded onto a train of waiting wagons destined for the Shanghai tunnels, home of the Exiles.

"Is all of that ours?" Sandi asked, gaping at the convoy.

"That's just the tip of the iceberg. We sent some ahead, and the rest is still coming," Ric said with a huge grin. "Callum, O'Neill, and I had a very lucrative expedition. We discovered a gold mine's worth of loot to the northeast. Entire cities untouched except by nature."

"Impressive," Sandi said, watching the scene from the side-lines. "Are you going back?"

"O'Neill is in charge of that now. With help from the Zoo and us, of course. We will split whatever he finds," Ric explained.

"What does that mean for us?" Sandi asked.

"It means we can rebuild," Ric said with a broad smile.

"Rebuild? The tunnels?"

"Not the tunnels. The Zoo. We can rebuild it now, even bigger and better than before," Ric said, placing one ham fist on her shoulder. "We're going home, girl. We're going home."

Sandi stared at him, unable to reply. A knot of excitement unfurled in her chest. Like a desert bloom denied water for too long, hope blossomed when presented with the possibilities of what could be their new future. "You really mean that?"

"I do, and it will be a wonderful day for us all," Ric said. "But first, we need to get back to the tunnels. There's much work to be done."

"Of course," Sandi agreed, shouldering her bag.

Ric paused and eyed her with shrewd calculation. "Can I ask? Is this visit to the tunnels just that? A visit? Or are you coming home?"

"I... I don't know," Sandi admitted. "I thought it was a holiday, but now I'm not so sure."

"Well, think about it, girl. We need young, strong blood to rebuild. We need people like you and Paul. You know that's what your parents wanted for you."

"I know," Sandi said, chewing on her bottom lip.

"Remember. There's a seat on the council for both of you," Ric said. "Should you want it."

"Thank you. I'll think about it."

"You do that," Ric said with a brisk nod. "Now get off the boat and hitch a ride with a wagon. We don't have all day."

He rushed away, shouting orders as he hurried the workers along. Deck hands and soldiers alike.

Sandi looked around for Paul, but couldn't see him. He was lost in the hustle and bustle, so she did what Ric had suggested. She climbed off the boat and found a seat on the nearest wagon, squeezed in next to a couple of pallets.

"Are you comfortable, miss?" a young guard asked.

"I'm fine, thank you," she replied with a smile.

"Let me know if you need anything from me," he added, returning her smile.

"Ooh, someone likes you," David said, popping up next to her.

"No, he doesn't."

"Yes, he does," David teased. "You're a pretty girl. Why wouldn't he?"

Sandi blushed. David's words made her feel uncomfortable, but at the same time, it made her wonder. When was the last time she felt pretty? Like she used to before everything happened? General Sikes, losing her home, the Red Flux... all of it.

Prime's infirmary wasn't exactly conducive to a beauty routine. It was hard to feel good when you were covered in blood, vomit, snot, and other horrible bodily fluids.

That made her think about Ric's offer. It would be a very different kind of life from the one she'd envisioned. Instead of becoming a doctor and serving patients in a hospital, she'd become a leader and serve her people by guiding them into the future. Both options had appeal. The question was, which one should she choose? And what about Paul? What would he pick, given the choice? Prime or the Zoo?

Sandi shook her head and banished the thoughts. It was too much to think of all at once. Her mind was in a whirl, and she wanted to think of something fun. Something that didn't want to make her run screaming in the other direction.

She was mercifully distracted when the wagon started to move beneath her. With all the supplies unloaded, the captain and deck hands returned to their boat. They'd return to Prime for another cargo, and they also carried letters, messages, and other paraphernalia.

At the same time, Ric got the convoy moving. The entrance to the tunnels wasn't far. There were many secret entrances scattered in and around the old docks of Portland, but Sandi understood the haste. Out in the open, they were exposed and vulnerable to attack. Only inside the tunnels would they be safe.

Paul came looking for her moments later. He sagged with relief when he spotted her, and said, "Where were you? One minute you were on the boat, and the next you were gone."

"Sorry. I thought it best to get out of the way," she said, contrite.

"Don't do that again, okay? You scared me."

"Okay."

He walked next to her for a while, but she could see he was impatient. He kept craning his neck to look ahead, a cautious but hopeful look on his face.

"Go ahead," she said after a while.

"Are you sure?" he asked, failing to hide his eagerness.

"I'm sure."

"What about you?"

"I'm fine right here," Sandi said, waving around.

"Really?"

"Of course. I've got a comfy ride, and there are guards all around to keep me safe," Sandi said. "I'm right behind you."

Paul hesitated. "Alright. If you don't mind."

"Off with you," Sandi urged, waving him off.

With a grin, he ran to the head of the convoy, leaving her to her own devices. Sandi didn't mind. The winter sun was kind, warming her skin and making her feel lazy. The sky above her head was blue, and the wagon rocked from side to side as they traveled. The sensation was soothing, and her eyes soon began to droop.

The peace and quiet was not to last, however. The wagon behind hers was drawn by a camel, and the beast kept giving her the evil eye. It looked like a cantankerous animal, the kind she was well acquainted with from her time spent in the Zoo's stables. When it kept squinting at her, she cast around for something to use as a shield. Sure enough, it spat at her, the glob of saliva barely missing her head when she ducked.

"Hey, stop that," Sandi yelled.

The creature rumbled something in reply, clearly not as taken with her looks as the young guard had been. When it spat again, Sandi decided she'd had enough and jumped down. Dancing out of the nasty creature's way, she decided to walk the rest of the distance.

"Stupid camel," she cried, shaking her fist.

The beast grunted in reply and squirted a third glob of foul liquid in her direction. A final farewell.

Shaking her head, Sandi turned away. She hurried past the row of wagons, carts, animals, and drivers. The entrance to the tunnels beckoned, and she picked up the pace. *I wonder if my mom is there. And my dad. Do they know I'm coming?*

Halfway there, she spotted Paul. He stood next to the opening, facing off against two people. They had to be his parents, and she hoped the reunion wasn't acrimonious. The last she'd heard, Paul's father was still locked up. All because he didn't agree with the council and Moran and tried to stage a coupe. The attempt failed but the council was not so forgiving.

The entire incident had been a bitter pill for Paul to digest. He'd worshiped his dad prior to the incident, and it was one of the reasons he ran off to Prime in the first place. Now he was back and his dad was no longer a prisoner but a free man. *I'd better get my ass over there.*

Sandi arrived in time to see Paul and his father embrace, and the tension leached from her bones. It was a stiff hug, and both wore somber expressions, but it was more than she'd expected. Far more.

"Oh, Paul. I'm so happy to see you," his mother cried, pulling him into a tight embrace.

"Me too, Mom. I've missed you both," Paul replied, hugging her back.

Sandi dashed away a tear, overcome by emotion. "Hi, Mr and Mrs Watkins."

"Sandi? You're here too?" Paul's mom said, releasing Paul. She gripped Sandi's hands. "Are you well, my dear?"

"Yes, ma'am," Sandi affirmed with a shy smile.

"Call me Audrey, please. I insist. You're not a child anymore, but a grown woman," Mrs. Watkins said, squeezing Sandi's fingers until they became numb.

"Um, okay… Audrey," Sandi said, feeling a little uncomfortable. To her, Paul's mother would always be ma'am or Mrs. Watkins. Not Audrey. This was the same woman who fed them cookies and milk as kids or scolded them when they were naughty.

"I'm so glad you two are still together. Childhood sweethearts and all," Mrs. Watkins said. "I remember when you were just a little girl in pigtails stealing strawberries from my garden."

"Mom," Paul said, rolling his eyes.

Sandi chuckled. I remember those days."

"Even then Paul was smitten over you. You were the prettiest girl in the Zoo according to him," Audrey gabbled.

"Mom, please," Paul said with a groan. "You're embarrassing me."

"Well, what do you expect? I'm just so happy to see you. It's been lonely, especially with Robert being in..." Audrey trailed off, and an uncomfortable silence fell over the small group.

"Lock-up," Robert said. "With me being in lock-up."

"Robert, don't," Audrey said, reaching out.

Robert shook his head. "No, it's alright. We need to talk about this. We can't keep hiding from it forever."

"Dad, it's okay," Paul said with a helpless look.

Robert held up a hand. "It's not okay. What I did was wrong, and I let you and your mom down. I believed it was the right thing to do at the time, but I was blinded by my ego, and it nearly cost me everything."

"Oh, Robert," Audrey said, bursting into tears.

Robert drew her into his arms. "I should've said this sooner, but I'm sorry. I'm sorry for the suffering that my actions cost you, and I hope you can forgive me."

"There's nothing to forgive. I'll always love you, Robert," Audrey said with a blubbery smile.

"I love you too, sweetheart."

It was a happy moment for all of them, but it wasn't meant

to last. People jostled them from all directions, wagons piled high with supplies creaked past, and someone called to Robert. "Watkins! We need some help over here."

"Sorry, guys. I need to go," Robert said. "Duty calls."

He hurried away, and Paul watched him go. "What does he do now, Mom?"

"He works on an electrical team. Ric arranged it after… after everything that happened."

"That was kind of him," Paul said.

"Indeed, it was," Audrey said, her voice faint.

"Are you okay, Mrs. Watkins?" Sandi asked, watching the woman closely.

"I'm fine, dear. Just a little overwhelmed." Audrey managed a weak smile. "I think I need to lie down for a bit."

Sandi exchanged worried looks with Paul. "Why don't you take your mom home? I'll catch up with you later."

"Will you be alright?" Paul asked.

"I'll be fine. Besides, my parents have to be around here somewhere," Sandi said, looking around.

"I think they're over there, dear," Audrey said, waving a vague hand around. Her eyes were glazed and she looked confused.

"Thank you, Mrs. Watkins," Sandi said, falling into old habits. "I'll see you later."

Paul led his mother away, and Sandi turned her attention to finding her own family. She didn't have to look long before she spotted her father, Christopher Green. "Dad, over here!"

"Sandi," he cried out, opening his arms.

She closed the distance and flung herself into his embrace, happier than she'd been in a long time. "Oh, Dad. I missed you so much."

"Me too, sweetheart," he said, blinking through the thick

lenses of his glasses.

"Where's Mom?"

"She's at home, preparing your room. You know how she is. Everything must be perfect," he replied.

"I know."

"Ever since Ric sent that messenger, she's been in a tizzy preparing for your arrival. She even roped Olivia into her plans," he added.

Sandi's eyebrows rose. "You're kidding."

"I wish I was," her father said.

"Have you seen David around?" Sandi asked, searching the crowd.

"I think Aret got hold of him. I'm sure they'll turn up somewhere," he said, offering her his arm. "Come. Let me take you home."

"Thanks, Daddy. I'm glad to be here," Sandi said, squeezing his hand. She leaned against him as they walked, secure in the knowledge that she was home at last.

Chapter 12 - Callum

Callum stared at the blueprints on the table, his keen gaze scanning the lines. It was a representation of Prime city, but with a number of additions and expansions. His mind ran over the figures, and he calculated the years, labor, and supplies it would take to make the proposed changes. "It will take at least five years, if not more."

"Yes, it will, and we will need a lot of supplies to accomplish the task, but I believe we can do it," Moran said. She'd changed her hair, braiding it down her back with two shaven strips above each ear. With her iron will, strong features, and athletic build, she presented a striking figure, and it was no surprise she was the council leader.

"Tell me more," Patti Fry said. "Those squiggly lines don't mean much to me."

"This is Prime Hotel. It currently houses the infirmary, several staff members, a library, and a cafeteria," Moran said.

"Yes, I know," Patti said.

"I propose we turn it into a community center," Moran said. "The infirmary will expand into a fully-operational hospital complete with a rehabilitation center, pediatrics, x-rays, laboratory, an optometrist, a dentist, and grief counselors."

"What about the staff?" Patti asked.

"We will keep the staff quarters, cafeteria, and the library," Moran said. "They just need to be restructured and organized."

"There have been requests for a daycare center, as well," Kat said, moving closer to the table. She was bundled up in several layers of clothing to ward off the cold, and her face looked pale beneath the red woolen beanie that covered her hair.

"Sit down, lass," Callum said, dragging a chair over. "Ye mustn't strain yerself."

"Thank you, my love," Kat said with a gentle smile, and his heart nearly leaped out of his chest. In his eyes, she was still the most beautiful woman in the world.

She sat down, and the meeting resumed.

"We can work a daycare into the plans," Moran said with a brisk nod. "We still have some available space to work with here."

"If it's going to be a true community center, there should also be a space for classes. A place where people can learn new skills and trades for free," Kat added.

Moran stared at the blueprints. "Now, that is something I didn't think of, and I should have. It's an excellent idea."

"Don't beat yourself up, Moran. You've had a lot on your plate lately," Patti said.

"Indeed, ye have, lass. Why not let us help ye?" Callum said. "Now that Bruce has taken charge of the Watch, I find myself with a lot of extra time on my hands."

"I wanted to talk to you about that," Moran said, pouncing on his offer like a raptor. "Bruce wants you to be in charge of the new trainees. We've opened up a proper training center, but there's no one to run it."

"Ye mean, teach the newbies how to fight?" Callum asked.

"In a nutshell, yes," Moran said.

"I don't know," Callum said, mulling it over. "What do ye think, Kat?"

"As long as you're still around to help me raise this baby, I don't mind at all."

"It's a job with regular hours," Moran assured Kat. "No standing watch in the middle of the night or attending to emergencies. That's Bruce's job now."

"Sounds good to me," Kat said with a shrug. "Callum?"

"I suppose I could help ye out. At least until ye find someone proper for the job," Callum replied, but Moran's victorious grin told him there would probably never be anyone else. The training center was his now. He didn't mind, though. It would keep him busy, and he'd still have time for Kat and the baby. The best of both worlds.

"What about the fields?" Patti asked.

"We've planted the winter crops, and they're coming along well, but I'd like us to expand out to the east. The earth is rich and will yield well," Moran said.

"We'd have to set up proper defenses first," Callum said.

"Yes, but Bruce is working on it. We've had an influx of new blood in the Watch," Moran said.

Patti snorted. "A lot of young ones want to get out from underneath their parents, and living in the barracks is the perfect way to do that."

"Aye, and its free board and lodging," Callum added. "Something, the poorer families sorely need."

"Which reminds me," Kat interrupted. "We should set up a soup kitchen and a thrift shop. We can ask for donations and volunteers to run it. A warm meal and clothes for all who need it, especially in winter."

"We can set that up here, next to the church. There's an

empty building in need of repair," Moran said, pointing at a spot on the blueprints.

"What about the rest of the city?" Callum asked. "How are things looking?"

"We're upgrading the various infrastructure as quickly as we can, but it will take time. It's taken years of neglect to get us to this point, and we won't fix it overnight," Moran explained. "But we've accomplished much already. Electricians are rewiring public spaces, streetlamps, and businesses as we speak. Engineers have cleared out the city wells, installed new pumps, and replaced old rotten pipes. Volunteers have cleaned up the streets, we've opened a park and playground, and two schools opened their doors this week."

Callum whistled. "Tis an impressive feat, lass."

Moran inclined her head. "I hope to open a home for the elderly next month and to start work on the new community center. Hopefully, O'Neill will return from his latest expedition with plenty of material for us."

"I'm sure he will," Callum said. "He sent a message, and it looks promising."

"I'm glad to hear it," Moran said.

"This is all good and well, but what about the people?" Kat asked. "Can we survive the winter? What about the sick and poor?"

"The recent influx of supplies has helped a lot," Patti said. "We have both O'Neill and Vancouver to thank for that. Our food stores are above fifty percent and should last us until the next harvest. Plus, we treated the Red Flux, and most of the city's population is back on its feet. We took heavy losses, however. Around thirty percent, maybe more."

Callum shook his head. "Tis a grave thing indeed. So many

dead."

"Which is why we need to give them hope," Patti said. "Lee and I plan to have a public wedding in the square as soon as we can arrange it."

Kat perked up. "That's a lovely thought, Patti! How can I help?"

"In any way you see fit," Patti. "We will rely heavily on volunteers and donations to make this a celebration for the entire city to enjoy."

"We can release a portion of the stores for a public celebration," Moran suggested.

"Aye, and I'm sure the business sector can arrange for stalls and such," Callum said.

"I'll check the hotel's storerooms for tables, chairs, and decorations. Senator Douglas was very fond of his public spectacles, and I'm sure I can find what we need to make this a spectacular event," Kat said with a smug smile.

"At least he's good for something now, the old bastard," Callum muttered.

Laughter did the rounds, and the atmosphere lightened. The idea of a public wedding was exactly what everyone needed after the ravages of the past few months. It would bring cheer to the masses and brighten up the city.

"Right, I think tis about covers it?" Callum asked once the buzz died down. "Is there anything else we need to discuss? I promised the missus a foot massage, and I dare not skimp on my duties."

"Indeed not, Sir or I will have your head," Kat replied.

"Ooh, lucky you, Kat," Patti said with a wink. "I wish my intended was so eager to please."

"It's all in how you ask, Patti," Kat said with a twinkle in her eye.

Patti laughed. "I'll remember that."

"You do look stunning, Kat," Moran added. "Motherhood agrees with you."

Kat smiled and laid one hand on her stomach. She was beginning to show and glowed with happiness. "I do believe it does."

"Anyway, I'm sure we've covered everything except the question of Vancouver and its Mayor," Moran said.

"What about it?" Callum asked.

"Now that they've granted us supplies, we can be sure they'll want something in return," Moran said. "Nothing is for free, no matter what they say."

"I agree," Patti said. "I say we gather what we can spare as repayment and keep it aside for when they come knocking. We should not be beholden to anyone, especially a city with superior numbers, forces, technology, and goods."

"What if they want to discuss trade or send more supplies?" Moran asked.

"I say we hold off until Rogue and Seth return. They should be able to tell us more about these people and their leader," Kat said.

"Agreed," Moran said. "I want to know who we're getting into bed with before we make a mistake."

"Aye, we can shift for ourselves now," Callum said. "'Tis the best way."

"I'll speak to Lee as well. Maybe he can shed some light on his former people," Patti said.

"Casey and the other Vancouverites have all gone, right?" Callum asked.

"Yes, they refueled their planes and trucks and took off a few days ago, and I'll admit I was happy to see them go. They are an unknown quantity in these uncertain times," Moran said.

"Aye. We need to be careful," Callum added.

"Alright, folks. That concludes today's meeting, and we'll reconvene a week from now," Moran said. "You all know what to do."

The gathering broke up as they all went their way, including Kat and Callum. He placed a protective arm around her waist and led her outside. After saying their goodbyes, they strolled back to the hotel at a leisurely pace.

It was a fine morning. The kind that made him think of the future and their place in it. "Can I ask ye a question, lass?"

"Yes, you can," Kat replied.

"Are ye happy with me?"

"How can you ask something like that? Of course, I'm happy with you," Kat said, stopping midstride to gaze up at him. "I love you, you big dummy. I always have, and I always will."

Callum grinned. "A big dummy, you say?"

"The biggest," Kat said, standing on tiptoe to press a kiss to his lips.

"Then ye'll marry me one day?" he asked.

"That depends," Kat said, a twinkle in her eye. She looped her arm through his and resumed their walk, dragging him along.

"Depends on what?" he asked, perplexed.

"On the way you ask," Kat said. "I expect to be swept off my feet."

"Err, and when do ye expect this occurrence?" Callum asked, his brow furrowed.

"Definitely not while I'm pregnant," Kat said with a stern look. "So you have plenty of time to plan the whole thing."

"Right. Got it," Callum said, his mind going into overdrive. "Tell me, lass. What's yer favorite flower?"

Kat laughed. "Oh, no. I'm not making it that easy. You'll have to figure this one out for yourself."

"Och, why do ye have to make it so hard?" Callum asked, though he secretly enjoyed being challenged.

"Because that's what we women do. We make you work for it," Kat said. "But we're worth it, right?"

Callum nodded and pulled her closer. "Yer worth every second, lass. Every single second."

Chapter 13

After their run-in with the quicksand, Ronan decided to call it quits for the day. It was too late to carry on, and both Seth and Rogue needed to clean up. They parked the vehicles on the nearest patch of dry land, circling the trucks for added protection from the creatures of the swamp.

In the middle, they built a bonfire and gathered enough wood to last the night. The wood was damp and created a lot of smoke, but it kept the insects at bay. While Rogue and Seth washed the gunk from their bodies and put on fresh clothes, Jessica, Bear, and Imogen prepared dinner. Ronan volunteered for the first watch, still not talking to anyone after the loss of Spook while Daniel and Lila wandered off, deep in conversation.

Clean and refreshed, Rogue chose a spot next to the fire and huddled close to the flames. The smoke stung her eyes and permeated her clothes, but she didn't care. She was happy as long as she was warm, whole, and free from bugs.

"Here you go, love," Seth said, passing her a plate of beans and smoked meat.

She took it with a smile of thanks, glad for the opportunity to fill her belly. The food was surprisingly good, flavored with dried herbs and tomato, courtesy of Bear's culinary expertise.

"Thank you, Bear. The food was excellent, as always."

"My pleasure, girly," he rumbled in reply.

"A man of few words," Jessica said, nudging him with her shoulder.

He grinned and nudged her back, and the two shared a warm look.

It gladdened Rogue's heart to see them so happy. It was easy to take Bear for granted. Silent and morose, he stayed in the background until his hammer was needed, but there was so much more to him than that. He was loyal, warm, loving, and a great cook. *He deserves happiness. He deserves love.*

Nigel sat down opposite her and eyed her with raised eyebrows. "You clean up well."

Rogue shrugged.

"For the record, I'm glad you're still alive."

"So am I," Rogue said. "And we have you to thank for it."

"It was nothing."

"It was more than that. Much, much more, and I owe you one," Rogue said. "We owe you one."

Seth nodded. "That we do."

"What's done is done. Forget about it," Nigel said.

At that moment, Lila and Daniel appeared from their walk and took their places beside the fire. They whispered to each other like naughty schoolgirls, staring at the others with sly grins.

Eyeing the couple with acute dislike, Rogue decided it was bedtime. Anything was better than spending time in their company.

"Goodnight, everyone. I'm tired," she said with a big yawn.

"Already?" Daniel asked with a smirk.

"It's not like you'll turn into a pumpkin at midnight," Lila added.

Rogue rolled her eyes but didn't reply. It wasn't worth the hassle. "Sleep well, Jessica. Imogen. Bear."

"I'll come with you," Seth said. Together, they climbed into the back of Jessica and Bear's truck, sleeping on a bed of blankets. It was pretty comfortable and beat sleeping in the front of their old truck. Both Jessica and Bear preferred sleeping by the fire, and Imogen slept in the front, so it was an arrangement that suited everyone.

"Wake me up when it's time for my watch," Rogue murmured, wrapped in the warmth of Seth's arms.

"We'll see, darling. Now sleep," he whispered, pulling her close.

She closed her eyes and drifted off into a deep, dreamless sleep, only to awaken with a gasp several hours later. The blankets next to her were cold and empty, the night outside dark and ominous. The hair on the back of her neck prickled, and her gut told her something was off. "Seth? Are you there?"

No answer.

"Seth? Please answer," she pleaded.

Still nothing.

Feeling around her in the dark, Rogue pulled on her boots and reached for her jacket, belt, and weapons. Armed and dressed, she slipped out of the truck and headed toward the front. A look through the window revealed that Imogen was still fast asleep on the front seat.

Reassured, Rogue headed toward the fire, a single point of light in the darkness all around them. A glowing bed of coals was all that remained, and she quickly added a couple of logs from the woodpile. The flames flared to life, and she felt a rush of relief as the night receded to a safe distance.

Rogue studied the camp. All was quiet, and everything seemed normal. Bear lay on his back with Jessica tucked into his side. They were both fast asleep, and she was careful not to wake them. Going from vehicle to vehicle, she searched for Seth.

Along the way, she passed Ronan's truck and spotted him huddled on the front seat with a blanket wrapped around him. The same applied to Lila, but she saw no signs of Daniel or Nigel. That bothered her a little, but they could be anywhere. On watch duty, taking a leak, or sleeping in the back of a truck like she and Seth did.

The person she cared about was Seth. He was gone, and she needed to find him, even if it was to reassure herself that he was okay. Ever since Spook got killed, she had nightmares of vicious man-eating crocodiles chasing her through the swamp. Seth knew this and started taking her watches for her despite her protests. That meant he got less sleep, and she was worried it would affect his level of alertness. The last thing he needed was to have something sneak up on him or to fall asleep at an inopportune moment.

Rogue picked her way through the vehicles toward the edge of camp. If Seth was on watch, that was where he would be. At the same time, her senses kicked into overdrive, and the further she moved away from the fire, the more nervous she got.

A low moan caused her to freeze in her tracks, and she sucked in a deep breath. Her heart thudded in her chest, a staccato beat that thrummed through her veins. Time passed by with only the sounds of the swamp around her until she thought she'd imagined it. Then she heard it again. The harsh groan of a creature in pain. No, not a beast. A man.

"Seth? Is that you?" Rogue whispered, afraid of what she might find. Another moan carried toward her on the cold breeze, accompanied by a scraping sound. A twig snapped, and she jumped, her stomach leaping into her throat.

Step by step, she moved toward the noise, her eyes sweeping the ground. The moon shone cold and bright above her head, its silver touch casting the barren swamp in hues of iron and gray.

A shift, a drag, a grunt of pain. That was the trail she followed. A picture formed in her head of an injured person dragging him or herself toward the safety of the camp. That raised a whole host of questions in her mind: Who was it? How did they get hurt? And what if whatever hurt them was still around to attack?

Rogue was tempted to call out for help or run back and fetch the others. The thought of running into a crocodile played to her worst fears, and her legs turned to jelly. But she resisted the urge to flee. What if she alerted a hostile animal or dinosaur? What if it finished the job while she fetched help? Scraping together the tattered remains of her courage, she pressed onward.

Ten yards.

Twenty yards.

Thirty yards.

Rogue looked back at the camp and gulped. If something attacked her now, she was on her own. Help would never arrive in time.

"S... someone... help me, please," a hoarse voice sounded.

The pitiful plea reached Rogue's ears, and she gasped. "Nigel?"

"Please... help..."

Rogue rushed forward and almost fell over his form, lying prone in the mud. One had lay stretched toward the camp while the other clutched his belly. A shaft of moonlight fell across his face, and his waxen skin shone pale against the collar of his jacket.

"Nigel, what happened?" she cried, dropping to her knees beside him.

"D… d…." He dissolved into a coughing fit

Rogue frowned. "Dinosaur? You were attacked by a dino?"

Nigel gasped for air, unable to reply. Bloody froth foamed on his lips, and she ran her hands over his chest and arms. It was difficult to see in the dark, but her hands came away wet and sticky.

Nigel convulsed, his body clenching into a ball. He gripped his stomach with both arms, and she leaned closer to get a better look. The awful truth dawned, and she jerked away with a horrified cry.

His stomach was ripped to shreds, and he was holding his entrails inside his belly through sheer tenacity. The ropes bulged between his fingers, pink, wet, and slimy. Streamers of torn skin and muscle added to the trauma, and the earth was soaked with his blood.

"Nigel, don't move. Lie still," Rogue cried, removing her jacket. She wadded it up and pressed it to his injuries. Positioning his hands over the thick material, she added. "Hold that while I get help, okay?"

"D… d…" Nigel's lips worked as he tried to get the words out. "Da…"

"Shh, don't try to talk. Save your strength. I'll be right back," Rogue said, preparing to jump up.

Nigel's stared at her, and his eyes widened. "W… watch…"

A sickening blow hit Rogue in the temple, and a pained grunt tore free from her lips. Her body went limp. A marionette doll whose lines had been cut. She fell to the ground, her face mere inches from Nigel's. As her vision faded to black, he spoke one last time, and the word reverberated through her brain like a gong.

"D... Daniel."

Chapter 14

A low growl reverberated through Rogue's skull. It competed with the throbbing headache that had taken up residence in her brain, and she struggled to focus. Blinking her eyes, she was alarmed to find her vision filled with black. *What's going on? Am I blind? I can't be blind!*

Every thought sent a fresh stab of agony through her head, and her adrenalin spiked. With a supreme effort, she shifted her head and tried again. Her lids fluttered open, and she stared into the dead eyes of Nigel. "Holy crap!"

A hoarse scream rang from her lips, and she scrambled backward as fast as her arms and legs allowed. Each movement sent a fresh volley of stabbing pains into her brain, and her head swam. "Nigel!"

But Nigel was beyond answering. He stared at her with a vacant expression, his life's blood soaking the earth on which he lay. Foam flecked his lips, and clods of dirt clung to his pale skin. Suddenly, he moved, and her eyes widened. *Is he alive? He doesn't look alive.* "Nigel?"

He moved again, his entire body shaking as if he were having a violent fit. Then she heard it again. A low, rumbling growl that sent a shiver up her spine and awakened an ancient primal fear within her soul. *What the hell is that?*

She edged away from Nigel's corpse, searching the area for the noise she'd heard. At the same time, she tried to keep quiet, but it was hard. Her body refused to cooperate, and her reflexes were sluggish. The cold didn't help. It leached into her bones and sucked the heat from her core. Lying in the icy mud had caused her body temperature to drop, and she tried to remember what had happened.

She didn't know. It was all a blur—a mess of jumbled memories that made no sense. There was no time to sort it out anyway. Not while she was in danger. *I have to get away.*

A clump of bushes blocked her path, and Rogue swore beneath her breath. Kicking backward, she forced her way through. Twigs and branches tugged at her clothes and scratched her skin.

It wasn't easy, but she persisted. In the distance, a faint yellow glow beckoned. The fire from camp. If she could make it back, she would be okay.

A beam of moonlight broke through the clouds above, and a pair of yellow orbs caught her attention. When they blinked, she realized they weren't orbs at all. They were eyes. Yellow, slitted eyes. *Crocodile!*

Her breath caught in her throat, and she froze to the spot. Mesmerized, she could do nothing but watch as a monstrous creature crawled from the bog. Each ponderous step brought it closer and closer, but she couldn't move. Its scaly limbs slithered across the wet mud, and a tail as thick as her body swept the ground.

Its enormous head swung in her direction, and panic flooded her veins. While she couldn't get a good look, she could tell the beast was gigantic. It dwarfed her in size, and she felt insignificant and puny.

Its throat vibrated, a deep growl rippling through the air. The monster pounced, its jaws stretched wide. Rogue acted on instinct and threw herself to the side. The croc's teeth snapped shut mere inches from her flesh.

Terrified, she cast around for a means of escape. The beast attacked again, and it snagged a piece of her jacket. Tossing its head, the creature threw her several feet through the air. She hit the ground with a terrific thud, unable to breathe, let alone think.

Lying on her back, she stared up at the stars. It would be so easy to give up. Her head hurt, her body ached, and she was so cold. So cold. But she couldn't give up. She had to keep trying.

Rogue tore off her jacket and tossed it at the croc with dogged determination. It snapped up the garment and shook it like a ragdoll. With the beast distracted, she made her escape. A low rock and a thorny bush provided refuge, and she scrambled behind them. Hunkered down low, she waited.

The croc ripped the jacket to shreds before it lost interest. Dropping the torn material, it swung its head from side to side. Its nostrils flared wide, and Rogue held her breath. Thankfully, her scent was disguised by a layer of muck and slime.

The prehistoric reptile cast around for a few more seconds before it gave up. It headed straight for Nigel, drawn by the stench of blood. It bit down on the man's torso, and the sternum snapped with a loud crack. Tendons and flesh tore as the beast dragged the corpse deeper into the swamp. It soon reached a stretch of water and disappeared into the murky deep with a splash.

Released from her frozen state, Rogue jumped to her feet. A white light flashed across her vision, followed by a wave of nausea. It hit her in the stomach, and a flood of bile rushed up her throat. She tried to fight it, but it was impossible. Burning liquid sprayed from her lips, and she struggled to remain upright.

Determined to get back to camp, she focused on the fire, its light a beacon in the night. It called out with its promise of life and warmth. If she could only get to it, she'd be safe. Suddenly, a single word flashed through her brain, and she stopped abruptly. *Daniel.*

White-hot rage infused Rogue's mind, clearing away the fog of confusion that had her in its grip. "That scheming jackal."

Daniel killed Nigel, and it was he who hit her in the head and left her for dead. And what about Spook? Was it possible? Did he kill the boy as well?

Rogue shook her head, horrified. All this time, they were traveling with a murderer in their midst. And what about Lila? She was always at his side. Was she in on it too?

Gritting her teeth, she yanked the gun from her hip holster and checked the load. Her hands were unsteady, and her head swam, but she didn't give a damn. "Time to find out what the fuck's going on."

Rogue stumbled into the light, one hand pressed to her head. Like a drunkard, she swung around in a wild circle. "Daniel? I know you're here. Come out and face me, you coward."

Her foot hit a stack of pots and pans, and the delicate tower collapsed with a resounding crash. Another step caused the pile of firewood to roll into the coals, and sparks flew all over the place.

Jessica jumped up from her bed with a yelp, burned by a glowing ember. She grabbed her gun and looked around. When she spotted Rogue, she frowned, "What's with the racket?" Bear was right behind her, wielding his hammer like a caveman, and she placed a reassuring hand on his forearm. "It's okay. It's Rogue."

"Yes, it's just me," Rogue said, grinning like a maniac.

"What are you doing?" Jessica cried. "What happened to you?"

"Your head," Bear rumbled, reaching out to her with one hand. "Blood. Too much blood."

"Don't worry about my head, Bear," Rogue said. "I'll be alright."

He growled. "Who hurt you?"

"You'll see."

The next moment, Seth stormed into the light. When he saw her, his expression turned to horror. "What happened to you? You're covered in blood. Are you hurt?"

Rogue touched her temple and winced. "I got knocked on the head." She stared at the blood on her fingers, fascinated by the crimson sheen.

"Let me help you," Seth said, moving toward her.

"No, wait right there. I'm fine for now. First, I have a job to do," Rogue said, holding up her free hand.

"Job? You're not making any sense," Seth said. "Let us help you, please."

Rogue shook her head. She didn't feel right. Her brain was fuzzy, and nothing seemed to work right, but she knew one thing for sure. She had to make Daniel talk. "Forget about me. Where's Daniel?"

"Daniel? I relieved him on duty earlier, but I haven't seen him since," Seth said with a look of confusion.

"I'm here," Daniel said, appearing like a ghost from the night. Lila shadowed him, her eyes hooded and watchful.

"What's going on here?" Ronan said, popping up behind

Seth.

A sleepy-looking Imogen stood behind him, rubbing her face. "What's with all the noise?"

"That's a good question," Daniel said. "I believe Rogue was about to enlighten us."

"You killed Nigel, you monster," Rogue cried, pointing her gun at Daniel.

Imogen gasped and pressed both hands to her mouth. "What?"

Daniel held up both hands in a gesture of self-defense. "Whoa, there. I didn't do anything of the sort. Where's Nigel?"

"Right where you left him. Or at least, what's left of him after the crocodile got him," Rogue yelled.

"Where I left him? I didn't touch him," Daniel said, as cool as ice.

"You can't fool me. I know it was you. He told me before he died," Rogue said. "And then you tried to kill me too."

"Is that true?" Seth said, turning to face Daniel.

"Of course not. She's crazy," Daniel said, laughing. "I mean, look at her. She's off her rocker."

"She's not crazy," Imogen said, speaking up. "She's hurt."

"You stay out of this, little girl," Daniel snarled.

Imogen shrank back, placing herself behind the nearest truck.

"Leave her alone, and I know exactly what I'm talking about," Rogue said with a snarl. "You killed Nigel."

"Rogue, wait. Have you got any proof?" Ronan asked, holding out one hand to her.

"Proof? I've got Nigel's last words," Rogue said.

"She's lying. She killed Nigel, and now she's trying to cover her tracks," Lila shouted, pointing an accusing finger.

Rogue swung the gun toward Lila and bared her teeth. "I wondered how long it would take for you to show your true colors."

"You stupid girl," Lila said with a hiss. "What do you think you're doing?"

"Tell me, Lila. What did you find in the mayor's office? What information was so valuable that you'd murder all of us to keep it to yourselves?"

"You don't know what you're talking about," Lila said.

"Rogue, I trust Daniel and Lila with my life. They would never betray me," Ronan said.

Rogue fixed him with a glare. "Then you're a fool, and I'll prove it."

"No!" Ronan shouted, but it was too late.

Taking swift aim, Rogue shot Daniel in the leg. He dropped to his knees with a scream of pain, clutching the leg. "You crazy bitch!"

"No!" Lila screamed.

"Admit it. Admit you killed Daniel and tried to kill me," Rogue said, relentless. The sight of his pain aroused no pity. Rather, she felt feverish and unhinged. *Maybe's he right. Maybe I am crazy.*

"Rogue, what are you doing? This is not the way to handle things," Jessica cried.

"Stop it!" Ronan yelled.

"Rogue, please," Seth said. "Let's talk about this."

She ignored them all, the memory of the crocodile cracking Nigel's sternum before dragging him off still fresh in her mind. Rage mixed with revulsion filled her mind, and she fixated on Daniel with gruesome intent. *I will make him talk, no matter what.* "Tell the truth, or it's your other leg, Daniel."

"You're crazy." He spat on the ground and bared his teeth. "I'll get you for this."

"Admit it," Rogue screamed, her voice raw. "You know you did it. I know you did it."

"Fuck off," he replied.

"Fine," Rogue said, cocking her head. "I guess we're doing this the hard way."

She shifted her aim to his other knee, and his eyes grew large. "No, wait. It wasn't me, I swear it. I never even went into the swamp tonight. I've been inside the camp with Lila the whole time."

"I don't believe you," Rogue said, squeezing the trigger.

"If you never left camp, then why are your boots so muddy?" Seth asked in a quiet voice.

Rogue blinked, and her fingers eased off the trigger. "Good question. Answer him."

Daniel stared at them, caught off guard. "There's mud everywhere. We've been traveling all day. Sometimes we stop and catch a break."

"That mud is fresh, and it's black. There's no mud like that around here," Jessica pointed out.

Daniel's mouth worked, but not a sound came out.

"This is ridiculous. He was with me all night," Lila said, raising her chin.

"Was he? Because your shoes are clean," Jessica said.

"Lila? Daniel? What's going on here?" Ronan asked.

"I told you. Nothing," Daniel insisted. "She's lying."

Ronan stared at him with a stark expression. "I trusted you. I trusted both of you."

Before Daniel could open his mouth, Lila yanked the gun from his belt and swung it around the clearing. "Screw you.

Screw all of you. We don't need you. We'll be richer than the mayor once we sell what we know to the highest bidder. Richer than all of you!"

Daniel's head drooped. "Lila. Why did you do that?"

"Because we don't need them. We never did. I only agreed to wait because you insisted on picking them off one at a time," she added. "Now, I'm taking matters into my own hands." She pointed the gun at Rogue. "Starting with you."

"Not if I kill you first," Rogue said, aiming for the center of Lila's forehead.

Lila sneered. "We'll see about —"

Bear hefted his hammer and threw the weapon at Lila. It swung end over end through the air, the outcome inevitable. With a sickening crunch, it hit Lila in the chest. Her ribcage exploded, and blood burst from her lips. She dropped to the ground without making a sound and collapsed to the earth like a shattered doll.

Daniel stared at Lila's ruined body with shock. Directing an accusing gaze at Bear, he said, "You killed her."

Bear didn't reply. He simply folded his arms across his chest.

"You'll be sorry," Daniel said, his shock turning to rage. Before Rogue could make a move, he launched himself at Lila, yanked the gun from her hand, and shot at Bear. Several bullets whizzed through the air, most of them going wild. Once grazed Jessica's arm and another clipped Bear on the hip. Imogen screamed and ducked down behind a truck, unscathed.

Daniel's rampage ended when a single bullet punched into his forehead. He slumped to the ground, the gun falling from his nerveless fingers. He toppled over next to his lover, Lila, their limbs intertwined in death. As quickly as it began, it was over.

Chapter 15

Rogue blinked at the scene, unable to believe it was the end. Seth took the gun from her grip and led her to the fire. He made her sit down on a stump and examined her head. "This is deep. You need stitches, and you have a concussion."

That made her chuckle, and she looked at her fingers. Finally, she held up four. "Concussion number three, right?"

"That's four, babes," Seth said, looking more and more worried.

"Four concussions?"

"Four fingers. Now don't move," he said.

"I won't. I'm too tired to move," Rogue said, her eyes drooping. Now that the excitement was over, she felt drained of all her vitality. It leached from her bones, replaced by a cold that went bone-deep. Her teeth chattered, and her body shook.

Seth wrapped a blanket around her shoulders and rubbed her arms. "Don't you dare fall asleep on me. You have to stay awake. Promise."

"Why?"

"Just do it," Seth said, stoking the fire until it blazed into a bonfire.

Heat filled the clearing, and Rogue leaned toward the flames, soaking in the warmth. "That feels good."

"Stay awake!"

"Alright, alright," Rogue said, stretching her eyes open as far as possible.

"I'll help her," Imogen said, appearing by her side.

She sat down next to Rogue and talked. A nonstop stream of conversation designed to keep Rogue awake. At the same time, she rubbed Rogue's hands and feet to restore circulation.

Seth never stopped moving either. He tore a piece of material from his shirt, wadded it up, and pressed it to Rogue's head. "Hold this to stop the bleeding."

"Ow," Rogue complained, but she obeyed when he gave her the evil eye.

Next, he filled the kettle with water and put it on to boil. "Jessica? I need help over here. Where's the med-kit?"

"In the truck," Jessica said, examining the wound on Bear's hip.

"Here. Take mine. It's fully stocked," Ronan said, handing her the bag he'd fetched from his vehicle.

"Thanks," Jessica said. "You're a lifesav—" She stopped mid-sentence and stared at a red spot blooming on his shirt.

He followed her gaze. "Ah, damn. I thought I got off easy compared to the rest of you."

"You've been shot," Jessica said rather unnecessarily.

"It would appear so," Ronan agreed with a wry smile, seemingly amused. His knees buckled, and Jessica caught him before he hit the ground. Bear jumped in and helped her carry him to the fire. They propped him up against a stump and lifted his shirt.

Jessica stared at the bubbling wound in his abdomen, her hands growing still. The blood was black, and she lifted her gaze to Ronan's. "I... I'm sorry."

117

"You can't save me this time, Jess," Ronan said with a half-smile.

"No, I can fix this," she said, shaking her head.

"It's my liver, Jess. There's nothing you can do for me out here," Ronan said. "There's nothing anyone can do for me now."

"No! This can't be happening," Jessica cried out with fierce denial. She grabbed the med-kit and plugged the bullet hole with gauze and antiseptic. Afterward, she wrapped a bandage around his waist and gave him a shot of antibiotics followed by painkillers.

Rogue watched the scene unfold with a mixture of sorrow and regret. She was sorry for Ronan, just like she was sorry for Nigel and Spook. They didn't deserve such an end.

"If we can get you to Vancouver on time, they can operate," Jessica said, still working as fast as she could.

"I'll never make it in time, Jess," Ronan said, sweat beading his forehead.

"Yes, you will. We just need to get you to a truck," Jessica insisted. She tried to lift him to his feet but stopped when he screamed. Fresh blood soaked the dressing on his wound. It leaked onto the ground, thick, black, and sluggish.

"It's over, Jess," Ronan said. "You have to let me go."

"No."

"You always were a sore loser, but you can't win this round."

"Losing sucks," Jessica replied.

"I know. I lost to you once before, remember? Back with the Tarbosaurus?"

"I remember."

"Now it's your turn. We can call it even."

Jessica snorted. "If you can call dying getting even."

"I always win in the end," Ronan said with a weak grin.

Jessica sagged to the ground, defeated.

"Look after yourself and your friends. You're hurt."

Jessica glanced at her arm. "It's just a graze."

"It doesn't matter. An infection will kill you in the blink of an eye," he said. "Humor me, please."

"Fine," Jessica grumbled, reaching for the kit. Moving like an automaton, she disinfected and bandaged Bear's hip before moving onto her arm.

Rogue noticed and sat up straight. "Is it bad?"

"He got burned, that's all," Jessica said. "It's nothing serious."

"What about you?"

"A graze."

"I'm sorry," Rogue said, blinking like an owl. "I didn't want anyone to get hurt. The plan was to get Daniel to confess."

"Plan? Who cares about your plan, Rogue? Look at what you've done," Jessica cried. "Two people are dead, and another one is dying."

"I... I'm sorry. I didn't mean for any of this," Rogue said, shrinking back in the face of Jessica's wrath.

"Jessica, please," Seth said.

"No, Seth! She should've come to us first, instead of going off like a half-cocked gun," Jessica said.

"It's not her fault, Jess," Ronan said, reaching out to take her hand. "Look at her."

"I am looking at her, and I'm pissed!"

"No, I mean really look at her," Ronan insisted. "She's hurt badly, Jess. She's confused and disoriented. She needs your help."

"I can't help her. Not when you're dying because of her," Jessica said.

"That's on Daniel, and he paid for his crime," Ronan said. "She's not to blame."

"He's right, Jessica," Seth said. "Rogue's not thinking straight, she's got a concussion, and she's hypothermic. She must've been lying out there in the cold for quite some time."

Bear shook his head, his expression somber. "It's Daniel's fault. Not Rogue's."

"Tell us what happened, Rogue," Ronan said, shifting into a better position. "I don't know about Jess, but I need to understand."

Rogue nodded, relieved for a chance to tell her side of the story. She started at the beginning, careful to leave nothing out. Finally, she shook her head. "He told me. He made sure I knew who killed him, and I had to get justice for him."

"It's okay," Seth said, squeezing her shoulder.

"No, it's not. I know I went about it wrong, but I was so angry. When that crocodile took Nigel, it reminded me of Spook. Then I thought of all of you ending up the same way, and I couldn't stand it."

"That's awful," Imogen said, squeezing Rogue's hand.

"When I saw Lila and Daniel together, it all clicked. Whatever she found in the mayor's office was valuable enough for them to kill us all. Even you, Ronan."

Ronan coughed, and bloody sputum bubbled from his lips. "If this is anyone' s fault, it's mine for trusting Daniel and Lila."

"It's not your fault, and it's not Rogue's either," Jessica said with a sigh, handing Seth the med-kit. "We should search their bags."

"Later," Seth said, taking the kit. "First, we look after our own."

"I'll make coffee," Imogen offered. "I'm sure we could all use a cup."

Rogue perked up at the offer. "That does sound nice."

"Coming right up," Imogen said with a bright smile. A ray of sunshine in the dark.

"Let's see what we've got here," Seth said, examining Rogue's head.

She submitted to his touch, not complaining even when he hacked away half of her hair. The red locks fell to the ground where they writhed like snakes in the light of the fire. She blinked at the strange sight. *It's almost like they're alive.*

"Rogue, snap out of it," Seth said, shaking her shoulder.

"Huh? I'm fine," she said, trying to focus.

"No, you're not. This is one ugly gash."

Jessica stood up to investigate and winced. "The blow was hard enough to scrape the bone, but it's not cracked. You're lucky."

Rogue winced when Seth splashed antiseptic over the cut and stitched it up. "I don't feel lucky right now."

Jessica rummaged in the med-kit and removed a syringe. She gave Rogue the same concoction she gave Ronan: A mixture of antibiotics and painkillers. "That should take the edge off."

"Thanks," Rogue said, relieved to feel the stinging pain recede.

Ronan was not so lucky. He broke into a hacking cough, and Jessica rushed to his side. "How do you feel? Are you okay?"

"Honestly? It hurts like hell. I just want this over with."

"I've given you the strongest stuff we have, but I can give you more," Jessica said.

"No. Save it. It won't be long now," he said, leaning back with a grimace.

"I wish I could do something. Anything."

"You've already done more than you should, Jess. It's just a matter of time," Ronan said.

Rogue watched the scene unfold, wishing she could help. Then, inspiration struck. "Jessica, tell us the rest of the story."

"Story? What story?"

"The story of how you and Ronan became friends. You never told us the rest," Rogue said.

"Now's not the time," Jessica said with a frown.

"Why not? I love stories. Especially ones with me in it," Ronan said.

"Don't be stupid," Jessica said.

"It'll take my mind off the pain," Ronan coaxed.

Jessica sighed. "Fine. I'll tell the story, but no interruptions."

"Deal," Rogue said, and the rest nodded.

"Well, then. Here goes," Jessica said, settling down. "We were faced with an ocean of grass, hunting a fearsome predator: The Tarbosaurus."

Her voice lowered to a hypnotic drone, and silence fell across the camp as everyone moved closer to listen. Even Ronan's pinched expression relaxed as she told the tale, and soon, the swamp and its horrors faded into the background.

Chapter 16 - Jessica

"Ready?" Jessica asked.

"Not really," Lucia said. "But I'll stick with you and finish the job."

"Me too," Dean said.

Frodo swallowed hard, and his adam's apple bobbed up and down. "Okay."

"What a bunch of troopers," Ronan said with a mocking grin. "Lead the way, Jess. I mean, Jessica."

Jessica ignored Ronan and ducked into the sea of grass. It closed around her like a prison, and her field of vision shrank until she didn't know which side was up or down. Realizing her mistake, she backtracked. Once in the clear, she shook her head. "We can't go in there without some way to navigate. It's impossible."

"What do you suggest?" Ronan asked, not acting quite so cocky anymore.

Jessica smothered a grin, pleased to see him being a little more cautious. He was no fool, after all. Their lives depended on the success of the hunt. She fixed Frodo with a stern gaze. "I need you to act as our guide in there."

"How?" he asked.

"Get up there and make a fire," she said, pointing at a rocky outcrop covered with thorny brush and trees. "We can use the smoke to guide us back here should we get lost or disoriented."

"Is it safe?" Frodo asked with a doubtful frown.

"It's safer than whatever is in there," she said, pointing at the grass. "Besides, you've got a gun. If you get into trouble, shoot, and we'll come running."

"Okay," he said, trying to hide his relief.

Not for the first time, Jessica wondered why he'd volunteered for the hunt. *Did he think this was going to be easy?*

"Okay, well. See you later," Frodo said, shuffling toward the rocky outcropping.

Jessica watched with growing impatience while he climbed toward the top. Once there, he leveled a spot, gathered a few armfuls of wood, and started a fire. Finally, a thin streamer of white smoke lifted into the air like a beacon. "Thank the stars. I thought he'd never get it done."

"You and me both," Ronan muttered. "Can we go now?"

"Yes, we can," Jessica said, stepping into the thick stand of grass. "Remember, we have to stick together, but if you get separated, head toward the smoke. Got it?"

"Yes, ma'am," Dean said.

"Got it," Lucia added.

A grunt was all she got from Ronan. Not that she cared. *I hope the Tarbosaurus gets him. That would solve all of my problems.*

The stalks rustled above her head as she walked, a constant whisper of sound that she found both disorienting and distracting. It made it tough to listen to anything else, and she had to focus twice as hard.

They pressed onward, and the grass parted before them with reluctance. Step by step, they were drawn deeper into a maze of colorless death. A cloud of midges swarmed around them, attacking man and woman alike. Jessica slapped at the vicious creatures, cursing when they bit her exposed skin until it turned raw.

The sweat made it worse. Despite the season, it was hot inside their prison, and no hint of a breeze offered any relief. The sun rose high above their heads, its molten visage blazing down. It didn't take long before sweat burst from her pores, and the sting of salt became a constant irritation.

"Man, it's hot in here," Ronan complained.

"You're telling me," Dean said, reaching for his canteen.

"Be careful with that," Jessica cautioned. "We don't know how long we'll be out here."

Ronan snorted. "We'll be home by nightfall. I'm not staying out here in the dark."

Jessica didn't deign to reply. What was the point? The man had no brains and zero savvy.

It wasn't easy to follow the Tarbosaurus' trail either. Its stride was long, so each footprint had to be hunted down with care. If they lost it, they'd never find it again.

"Damn this grass," Jessica muttered, wiping the sweat from her brow. She removed her jacket and tied it around her waist. A couple of swigs from her canteen refreshed her, and she continued the hunt.

"Come on. guys," she urged when Lucia and Dean flagged. "We have to keep going."

"Can't we take a break?" Dean asked. "My legs feel like jelly."

"Stop complaining," Jessica muttered.

Ronan pulled a face. "Don't let us lesser beings hold you back."

"Would you shut up?" Jessica said, growing exasperated. "What if the Tarbosaurus hears us?"

"If we haven't—"

A thunderous crash interrupted the budding argument, and Jessica whirled in the direction of the noise. "Oh, shit. It's coming."

She whipped the Rigby from her back and aimed, even though she couldn't see a thing in the tall grass. The ground beneath her feet shook and shuddered as several tons of dinosaur flesh pounded the earth.

Jessica swallowed hard, fighting to keep calm. If she panicked now, it was all over. Behind her, Lucia and Dan cowered with their useless rifles. Confronted with reality, they realized what they faced, and fear was written all over their features.

"Stand your ground," Jessica yelled. "Whatever you do, don't run."

To her surprise, Ronan backed her up. He stood next to her, wielding his rifle with cool precision. "Listen to her. If you run, you're as good as dead."

Lucia flashed them a terrified look but nodded. "Okay."

Dan broke out in a sweat, but he remained standing in place.

Relieved, Jessica looked back in time to see the grass open like the Dead Sea parted for Moses in the Bible. A fearsome set of jaws filled by rows of razor-sharp teeth loomed above her. Each ivory incisor was the size of her hand, and a pair of beady eyes glared at her from a height of easily twelve feet.

The Tarbosaurus looked exactly what it was: Five tons of pissed-off carnivorous appetite powered by mighty hind legs and equipped with claws and teeth made for rending flesh into nothing more than a bloody pulp.

Jessica shot first... and missed.

"Shit!" she yelled, chambering a second round and last round. While she had two more shots in reserve, she was unlikely to get the chance to use it.

Ronan fired the next shot, and he didn't miss.

The fifty-caliber bullet thudded into the beast's head with the force of a freight train. It smashed through bone and pulverized brain matter until the Tarbosaurus' skull was little more than a pudding bowl.

The creature crashed to the ground as its brain stopped sending signals to its muscles. It plowed through the earth, sending up a spray of dirt in every direction. It came to a stop mere inches from Jessica's feet, and its final breath washed across her legs in a warm, damp, fetid-smelling cloud.

Jessica swallowed hard on the knot in her throat. "Shit, that was close."

"You're telling me," Ronan said with a triumphant grin. "Excellent shot, wouldn't you agree?"

Jessica rolled her eyes. "Go ahead. Have your —"

A bellowing roar caught her by surprise, and the next moment she was flying through the air. She slammed into the ground and rolled several feet before coming to a stop. Shocked and dazed, she raised her head and looked back. A second Tarbosaurus loomed above Ronan, Lucia, and Dan. A fearful knot of humanity that quivered before a mighty beast of legend.

Jessica couldn't believe her eyes. *Another one? Holy crap, it's a breeding pair.*

She immediately cast around for her rifle and spotted it a few yards away. Crawling on her hands and knees, she scrambled toward it as fast as she could. If only she could reach it in time, but fate did not agree.

Ronan chambered a fresh bullet and raised his gun, but he was too slow. The beast snapped at him, its teeth closing around his arm and rifle with brutal force. With a toss of the head, the Tarbosaurus flung the man aside like he was garbage.

"Ronan!" Jessica cried, but the only answer she got was a stuttering moan. He was still alive, but his injuries had to be severe.

A crackle of gunshots sounded: Lucia and Dan.

Brief hope flared in her chest, but a glance showed her what she'd known all along. Their rifles were useless against a creature the size and might of a Tarbosaurus. All it did was annoy the beast even further.

It snarled at Dan, and its jaws closed around his torso. A single shake of the head was all it took to rend him to pieces. The remains of what used to be a man dropped to the ground with a meaty thud.

Lucia screamed, her voice high and shrill. The dinosaur eyed her with annoyance before a quick bite pulverized her skull like a ripe melon. Blood and saliva dripped from the creature's teeth, and Jessica knew it would come for her and Ronan next. The Tarbosaurus spotted her and charged. Five tons of flesh-eating horror was heading her way, and she had but seconds to spare. *Now!*

Jessica threw herself at the rifle and scooped it up into a kneeling position. Steadying one elbow on her knee, she aimed at the thundering behemoth. A gentle squeeze unleashed the hollow-point bullet, and it turned the Tarbosaurus' heart to mush. The beast roared with pain, its mortality a sudden fact as it slammed to the earth.

Closing her eyes, Jessica sent up a silent prayer of thanks. She jumped to her feet and ran toward Ronan, relieved to find him still alive. His right arm was a mangled wreck, but she could still save him. "Hold on, Ronan. I'll be right back."

"Hold on with what?" he said with a hoarse voice. "My hand's a bit the worse for wear."

"Oh, my God. I can't believe you can joke at a time like this."

"Why not?" he said with a pained shrug. "I'm still alive, aren't I?"

"Not for long if we can't slow the bleeding," she said.

"I trust you," he said with a bland smile.

Shaking her head, she retrieved Dan's belt, jacket, and gun strap. She used the belt for a loose tourniquet, wrapped the torn flesh with the t-shirt, and fashioned a sling with the gun strap.

"There you go," she said, sitting back on her heels. "Time to go."

"Do I have to?" he groaned. "The grass is so nice and soft."

"You're welcome to stay if you want. You'll have company soon enough," she said, looking at the sky.

"Err, I'd rather not," he said, struggling to his feet.

"That's the spirit," she said with a mocking smile.

Ronan pulled a face, and they began the long trek back home.

They hadn't gone far when he stopped and turned to face her. "Just one thing, Jessica."

"Yes?" she replied with wary caution.

"You're one hell of a shot, and you can shoot by my side any day," Ronan said, his tone light but sincere.

Jessica eyed him for a few seconds. Finally, she nodded. "You can call me Jess."

***

"We made it to Frodo's fire, come hell or high water. He fetched help, and Ronan was saved. Even better, he kept his arm which was a miracle on its own," Jessica said. "You always were a tough sonofabitch, weren't you?"

Jessica's gaze dropped to Ronan, a fond smile on her lips. But the man lay unmoving, his gaze fixed on the horizon. Only a shell remained of the man he'd been: Charismatic, charming, sarcastic, but most of all, loyal.

"He's gone. He's really gone," Jessica said, her heart broken. Ronan had been a good man, an excellent leader, and an even better friend despite his flaws.

Bear placed one ham fist on her shoulder. "Let's bury him and pay our respects. The man was a warrior."

An hour later, they buried Ronan next to Lila and Daniel. The graves were shallow, but they piled rocks and brush on top to deter scavengers.

Afterward, Jessica looked around. "What do we do now?"

"We finish what we started," Seth said.

"Seriously? Half of us are dead, and the other half injured." She gestured at Rogue. "Some of us are seriously hurt."

"That doesn't change the fact that Prime needs us. There are people back home who depend on us," Seth said. "I'll keep a close eye on Rogue, and she can stay in the truck from now on."

Jessica sighed. "Alright. If you're sure."

"We've come this far. We might as well go all the way," Rogue said, moving to stand next to Seth.

"Let's get a move on then. It's almost dawn," Jessica said, gathering her things.

They broke camp and set off for the research facility in a single vehicle. It made no sense to divide their numbers into separate trucks. They were stronger together, and they'd make it to the end that way.

Chapter 17 - Lt. Cummings

"Lead the way, Sergeant," Lieutenant Cummings said, waving a hand at the field. "Stick as far right as you can, and head for that rocky shelf."

"Yes, Sir," Sergeant Horton said, heading straight for danger. The second Humvee followed, sticking close to their tail.

Tomi's throat closed when they hit the grass, and his stomach turned into a ball of knotted tension. He clutched the binoculars with sweaty palms and stared at the herd until he thought his eyes would shrivel and dry up.

"How are we doing?" James asked, tossing the lieutenant a nervous look.

"So far, so good," Tomi replied. "The herd is quiet."

"For now," Linda muttered, her expression taut.

"Don't jinx it," James scolded, wrapping and rewrapping his fingers around the wheel.

Tomi blew out a nervous breath and raised the binoculars once more. He swept the field, looking for any signs of restlessness. "Just take it nice and easy."

"Aye, aye, Captain," James replied, but the joke fell flat in the stiff atmosphere.

The herd remained calm as they drove by. The wind was in their favor, and they kept to a low speed to not startle the dinosaurs. A Lambeosaurus stared at them, chewing on a mouthful of leaves and twigs, and an Ankylosaurus snorted through its nose. An Alamosaurus lumbered past, each step sending a shock of vibrations through the earth. It was scary but also awe-inspiring.

Lieutenant Cummings relaxed as the minutes ticked by without any mishaps. Maybe they'd catch a break for once. James kept the Humvees to a nice even pace across the field, and they drew closer and closer to the stony shelf with its promise of safety.

The moment they drove past the rocks, Tomi sagged into his chair. He felt much safer with the wall between them and the herd. "Nice job, everyone. But don't let your guard down. We're not out of the woods yet."

Suddenly, a giant shadow swept overhead, blotting out the sun. Tomi stiffened in his chair and looked at Sonja in the turret. "What the hell was that?"

"I... I...." Sonja stuttered.

"Spit it out, private!"

"It's a Quetzalcoatlus, Sir, and it's coming right at us," Sonja cried.

"Holy shit," Tomi yelled, a vision of the flyer flashing through his mind.

With a wingspan of over thirty feet, and a beak capable of running through a grown man, the pterosaur was a terrifying adversary. There was no fighting it. Only surviving it, and he calculated fast. "Open fire, Private Barnes. Keep that thing off us."

"Yes, Sir," Sonja said, obeying the command.

"Sergeant, step on it. Get us out of this damn field," Tomi added.

James jammed his foot on the gas and floored it across the clearing. The second Humvee sped up to keep pace and Private Chiang, their gunner, opened fire as well. With both trucks racing at full speed and the fifty calibers providing cover, he prayed they'd make it to cover in time.

"How's it looking, Private Barnes?"

"It's still with us, Lieutenant," she replied, shouting to be heard.

"Damn it!" Lieutenant Cummings hung out of the window and looked up.

The Quetzalcoatlus soared above the Humvees, its attention fixed on them with evil intent. Bullets whizzed past its form, but none hit the creature. Then a second volley tore through the membranes of one wing, and the flyer shrieked.

"Yes, that's it!" Tomi yelled, but his triumph was short-lived.

The Quetzalcoatlus folded its wings and dive-bombed the second Humvee. It plummeted to the earth faster than Lieutenant Cummings would've thought possible. The fifty calibers ran through ammunition faster than the speed of light, but through sheer shitty luck, missed the mark. Bullets trailed behind the monstrous bird like fiery streamers, each shot one millisecond too slow.

At the last possible moment, the Quetzalcoatlus opened its wings. It plucked gunner Chiang from his seat in the turret as if it were plucking fish from a barrel. Chiang screamed, the cry of a man lost before he even realized it. The flyer soared across the open field with a flap of its powerful wings, following the stampeding herd.

Stunned, Tomi stared after the retreating Quetzalcoatlus and its prey. Bitter knowledge welled up within his chest. The knowledge that not every battle could be won, and not every soldier would return home to their family. With a heavy heart, he reached for the radio. "Sergeant O'Brian. Over."

"Yes, Sir. Over," came the somber reply.

"As soon as we reach the safety of the trees, pull over. We'll have a vigil for Private Chiang. Over."

"Yes, Sir. Over," Irene replied.

"And Sergeant? I'm sorry for the loss of your man. Over," Tomi added.

"Thank you, Sir. Over and out."

Silence settled over the cab and Lieutenant Cummings sank into a brooding despair. It always hit him hard when he lost someone, but at that moment, it seemed even harder than usual. *I'm getting too old for this shit. It's about damn time I retired.*

Chapter 18 - Sandi

With her father leading the way, Sandi entered the Shanghai tunnels for the first time in months. The place was much as she remembered it, just quieter. The only traffic was caused by the convoy she'd arrived in, which soon died down. The animals were taken to the stables, the supplies were put in storage, the guards and workers returned to their posts, and peace was restored. Or was it something else?

The place had a derelict feel, devoid of the life and laughter she remembered. The tunnels echoed with the sounds of their footsteps, and yellow light bulbs flickered overhead. A few establishments showed signs of life: A blacksmith created tools in the molten glow of his forge. A group of seamstresses sewed new garments from bolts of cotton. Leatherworkers tanned the fresh hides of slaughtered animals and dinosaurs, while a shoemaker crafted boots from cured leather.

Guards were stationed at intervals, and the common room revealed a couple of senior citizens playing chess. A young lady herded a gaggle of pre-school kids into the schoolroom, and a couple of people shopped for necessities in the trade store.

Surprised by the lack of people, Sandi asked, "Where is everyone?"

Her dad faltered mid-step, his expression grave. "I'm not sure this is the right time to discuss it."

"Why not?"

"I don't want to spoil your homecoming. It's unfortunate."

"What do you mean, unfortunate?" Sandi asked, growing more and more perplexed. "Did something happen here?"

"Well, yes. The Red Flux happened."

"Yes, I know about that," Sandi said, still confused. Then it hit her. "Wait a minute, are you saying they're all… dead?"

"Dead or still recovering in the infirmary," her father said, his cheeks pale.

"How is that possible? So many people?" Sandi cried.

As if he were on autopilot, her father rambled off an explanation. "The Red Flux hit us right after it hit Prime. Despite the warnings, we had no time to prepare, and the disease decimated the population."

"Decimated? How many?"

"We lost almost forty percent of the population, especially among the women, children, and the elderly."

"Forty percent!" Sandi said with a gasp.

"That's right. It would've been more if it wasn't for that shipment of antibiotics from Vancouver."

"But forty percent?" she repeated, horrified to the core of her being.

"What about Prime?" he asked with a frown. "It stands to reason they would've lost as much if not more than we did. The population is larger, the city bigger and more crowded. Control would've been difficult, and quarantining nearly impossible."

"I know, but…." Sandi trailed off, thinking back to the height of the pandemic. The packed hallways of the infirmary with the sick spilling over into the hotel itself. The lack of treatment, the desperation as the daily body count grew, and the mass cremations.

"I suppose we did lose as many as you did. Maybe more," she whispered, a shudder running down her spine. For the first time, she allowed the devastation of the past few months to hit her. To truly sink in.

"You saw it?" her father asked in a gentle tone of voice. "I heard you volunteered as a nurse."

Sandi nodded. "I wanted to help. I wanted to become a doctor. I wanted… I wanted so many things."

"We all did, sweetheart. We all did," he said, taking her hand.

"What do we do now?" Sandi asked, feeling a little lost.

"We start over," her father said. "We did it after the Shift. We did it after the great famine of ten years ago, and we'll do it again."

"Thanks, Dad. I needed to hear that."

"I'll always be here for you, sweetheart. Remember that," he said.

"I will," she said, making a silent vow in her heart.

"But right now, I want you to forget all of that," her father said, waving a hand at a closed wooden door.

"Huh?" Sandi asked, confused.

He opened the door and ushered her in with a broad smile. The moment she entered, a row of happy faces greeted her with a chorus, "Surprise! Welcome home, Sandi."

Sandi gasped, a frisson of delight replacing the chill of earlier. "What is this? What's going on?"

"It's your surprise party," her dad said. "Your mom arranged it."

"A party for me?"

"Not just for you," her mother said, appearing at her side. "You, Paul, and David are the guests of honor today. They're already here waiting for you."

"Mom! I'm so happy to see you," Sandi cried, throwing her arms around her mother.

"I'm happy to see you too, sweetie. You look well."

"I feel wonderful," Sandi said, glowing with happiness.

"What about you and Paul? Are you still together?"

"Very much so, Mrs. Green," Paul said, popping up next to them.

"I'm happy to hear that," Sandi's mom said with a broad smile.

"Could I steal your daughter for a dance?" Paul asked.

"Of course, you can as long as I can have her all to myself later on. Deal?"

"It's a deal, Mom," Sandi said, allowing Paul to usher her away.

He led her to Aret and David, who stood in a corner. Aret squealed and threw her arms around Sandi, babbling about everything she'd missed while she was gone. Sandi responded in kind, and it became a war of words which the boys watched with some amusement.

"Do you think they'll remember all of that tomorrow?" David asked.

"Definitely. Sandi never forgets a thing. It doesn't matter how long ago I did something wrong; she'll always bring it up when we fight," Paul said with a laugh.

"Well, someone has to remember the important stuff," Sandi said, chucking him on the arm.

"Exactly," Aret said, flipping her hair like she always did when she made a point. "It's up to us women to keep order in all of this chaos."

"Pfft, whatever," David said, flapping a hand through the air.

Aret pouted, and the two started bickering like old while Sandi and Paul were forced to pick sides.

For a brief moment, it felt as if nothing had changed. They were still together, and still friends, just older and wiser. Then Sandi spotted Jamie, Britanny's mom, and the world came crashing down around her ears.

"Have you spoken to her yet?" Sandi asked of David.

He nodded. "It was not easy, but she needed to know the whole story."

"Are you going to talk to her?" Paul asked.

"I have to."

"Do you want me to go with you?"

"I'll be okay," Sandi said, sucking in a deep breath. As much as she wanted to avoid the situation, she knew she couldn't and made her way across the room.

"Sandi? Is that you?" Jamie exclaimed.

"It's me. Alive and kicking," Sandi said. Then the smile on her face froze when she realized what she'd said. Appalled, a stream of words tumbled from her mouth, and she was powerless to prevent it. "I… I'm sorry. I didn't mean it like that. I miss Britanny so much, and I'm so scared you'll blame David and me for her death. She was so brave. The best of us. We —"

"Sandi, it's okay," Jamie said, gripping her hands tightly.

"It is? Are you sure? I —"

"I'm sure, Sandi. I miss Brittany more than words can say, and I wish she'd never left, but it was her decision. Not yours. Not David's. She did what she thought was right, and in the end, she saved her friends' lives. I can't ask for more than that. I'm just thankful I had her for as long as I did."

Jamie's words released a floodgate of grief within Sandi, and her face crumpled like wet tissue paper. "I'm so sorry."

"I'm sorry too, my dear. But we have to celebrate Brittany's life, not mourn it," Jamie said, pulling Sandi into a fierce hug.

"I know, and I'll try," Sandi said.

Jamie released Sandi and handed her a handkerchief. "I know you will."

Sandi wiped her tears away and managed a shaky smile. "Thank you for everything."

"It's nothing, dear. Now enjoy your party. You are young and strong and healthy. Your whole life is ahead of you. Live it."

For the rest of the night, Sandi remembered Jamie's words and tried to do them justice. She caught up with old friends, made dinner plans with her parents, and made shopping plans with Aret. She enjoyed the good food, even better company, and danced until her feet hurt.

Most of all, she basked in the glow of Paul's love. He was the linchpin around which her life revolved, and who knew how long she'd get to have him? All she could do was to be thankful for every moment they had together, and that would be enough.

Chapter 19

Rogue clung to her seatbelt as the truck rumbled across the final stretch of open ground. Dead leaves, twigs, and mulch squelched beneath the tires, and the worn shocks hit every rocky outcrop with the force of a hammer blow.

Imogen lay curled up on the seat next to her, her head resting on Rogue's shoulder. She was fast asleep, too exhausted to stay awake even with the bumpy ride. Seth sat on the other side, his expression somber as he stared out the grimy window.

He wasn't the only one. They were all shell-shocked and worn to the bone, their nerve-endings exposed to the cold touch of their grim reality. Half of their party was gone. Dead. Lost in the blink of an eye. Worst of all, some of them had deserved it.

Bear yanked the wheel to the right, swerving around a hole in the ground, and Rogue hit the window hard enough to set her teeth on edge. She didn't complain, though. The sooner they got to their destination, the better. Hopefully, they'd be able to rest, recoup, and lick their wounds.

Disturbed by the sudden change in direction, Imogen shot awake with a gasp. She sat upright and stared around her in shock. Her hair had escaped from its bonds and curled around her head like a fiery halo. "What's happening? What's going on?"

"It's okay. You can relax," Rogue said in a soothing voice. "We just hit a pothole."

"No, we didn't," Bear disagreed, speaking for the first time that day. "We missed it."

"You know what I mean," Rogue said, waving him off.

Imogen sank back against her seat with a gasp of relief. "Thank goodness. I don't think my heart could handle any more stress today."

"You and me both, sweetie," Rogue said. "Now, try to calm down. Take a deep breath. In and out."

Imogen obeyed, and soon, she was herself again. Or as close as it was possible to get under the circumstances. Somewhat reassured, Rogue turned her attention to the road ahead. She didn't want to think about anything other than their destination. It was the only thing she was capable of focusing on without screaming her head off. "Does anyone know how much farther we have to go?"

"We're almost there," Jessica said from the front seat. Her voice was hoarse, and when her eyes met Rogue's in the rearview mirror, they were haunted.

Rogue nodded, her heart going out to her friend. In a way, she felt responsible for Ronan's death, but she also realized it couldn't have gone down any other way. From the moment they left Vancouver, their fates were sealed.

"How's your head?" Imogen asked, looking up at Rogue.

"It hurts." That was a lie. The pain went far beyond hurt. It felt like someone was stabbing her in the brain with hot pokers. To add to her misery, her leg throbbed where the flyer cut her, and she couldn't sleep because of the nightmares. Every time she closed her eyes, she was back in the swamp with the crocodile.

"Are you okay?" Imogen asked.

"I'm fine."

"Really? You can talk to me, you know. I'm your friend."

Like Ronan had friends? Backstabbing, treacherous, murderous friends? No thanks.

"Just know that I'm here for you whenever you need me," Imogen said. She was like a child tugging at a string, seeing how far it would unravel. Only the string was Rogue's soul, and she couldn't allow it to fall apart any further than it had.

"I know. Thanks," Rogue said, turning away. She could feel Imogen's disappointment, but there was no help for it. "Go back to sleep, sweetie."

"Okay," Imogen mumbled, laying her head down again.

Rogue looked at Seth, and their eyes met across the girl's form. It was like a physical touch—a knowing. Instantly, the weight on her chest lifted. It wasn't gone, but she could breathe again.

"Thank you." Rogue mimed the silent words.

"Always," he mimed back.

For the first time that day, she could relax, secure in the knowledge that she had Seth. With him by her side, she could face anything, no matter how bad it was.

"I've been looking through these papers we found in Lila's bag," Jessica said, shuffling through a pile.

"And?" Seth asked, his interest piqued.

"Rogue was right. She found evidence of research carried out under Mayor Finley's orders."

"What kind of research?"

"The damning kind that would get her kicked off her throne," Jessica said.

"Like what?" Imogen asked.

"Time travel."

The two words dropped into the cab like stones in a pond. Though small, the ripple effect had far-reaching consequences.

"She ordered scientists to research time travel?" Rogue asked, not sure if she heard right. "After what happened the last time?"

"That's right," Jessica said. "It's hard to believe, but it's all here."

"My God," Seth said, at a loss for words.

"I can't believe my mom would do such a thing. Why?" Imogen said, her expression stricken.

"I'm sorry, sweetie," Jessica said. "This is not the kind of thing you want to learn about your mother."

"No, it's not, but if it's true, she has to be stopped," Imogen said, her jaw setting into a stubborn line.

Suddenly, Rogue caught a glimpse of her mother in her. Only a better, softer, kinder version than Maeve Finley. *Someday, Imogen Finley will make a fine leader. All she needs is time.*

"I think we're here," Bear said, breaking into her thoughts.

Eager to see the research facility, she leaned forward in her chair, but there was nothing there. Nothing but wide open space. "What do you mean, we're here?"

"The map says so," Bear said.

Jessica took the map from him with a frown. "Let me see."

After a couple of seconds, she shook her head. "According to Maeve Finley's map, we're in the right place."

"But there's nothing here," Rogue protested.

"Not nothing," Seth said, his voice so low she had to strain to hear him.

"What do you mean?"

"Look at the trees, the vegetation, and the ground. This is a

144

blast site. Whatever used to be here is gone. Blown up."

Rogue stared at the field, noticing the blackened trees, brush, and scorched earth for the first time. It radiated outward in the circle, and there was a crater in the center. Dumbfounded, she sank back into her chair. "You're right. It's a blast site."

"And I bet the research facility sat right in the middle," Seth added.

"The research. It must've gone wrong," Jessica said, slowly shaking her head.

"She killed them. My mother killed these people," Imogen said, stricken.

Rogue reached out to pat her shoulder, but she couldn't offer more than that. The facility they'd come so far to find was gone, destroyed by the very science they'd pursued, and Maeve Finley was to blame.

"What do we do now? Go back?" Jessica asked.

"Yes, there's nothing for us here but death and destruction," Seth said.

"Can we take a break first?" Imogen pleaded. "I need to pee."

"Okay. Let's take a short break. It's a long way home, after all," Jessica said, opening her door. "And while we're here, we might as well see if there's anything left."

Rogue nodded and climbed out of the truck. She doubted they'd find anything. Not a brick remained standing. But she welcomed the opportunity to stretch her legs and breathe fresh air before she had to face her worst nightmare again: The inland sea.

Chapter 20 - Lt. Cummings

Tomi leaned forward in his seat, squinting into the distance. His eyes weren't quite as good as they used to be, and it was coming on to dusk. "What's that?"

"It looks like a vehicle, Sir," Sonja said from the turret.

"Is it our guys?" Tomi asked.

"Hard to say, but seeing as we're in the middle of nowhere, it's probably them," Sonja added with a hint of sarcasm.

"Haha, hilarious, Private Barnes," Tomi said, though her quip certainly lightened the mood. After their run-in with the Quetzalcoatlus, nobody was in the mood to laugh. *Let's hope the rest of the trip goes smoothly.*

"Sir?" Linda asked.

"Yes, Private Longo?"

"The research facility should be right there."

"Right where?" Tomi asked, looking at her over his shoulder.

"Right there where they are," she said, pointing at a map. "There should be a huge building right in the middle of that clearing."

Lieutenant Cummings looked ahead. "Are you sure? There's nothing there."

"This is getting weird," Sergeant Horton said. "Look at that."

Tomi looked where he pointed and saw a row of blasted trees.

The blackened trunks looked stark against the greenery of the forest, reaching to the sky with twisted limbs. "What in hell's name happened here?"

"There's more, Sir," James said.

Tomi studied the area, and the closer they got, the worse the destruction became. The torched skeletons of trees surrounded the entire field, and the grass looked like a bed of charcoal.

"It looks like a bomb went off here," Sonja said from her turret.

"This is not good. Where is that damn research facility?" Lieutenant Cummings muttered.

"I think this was the research facility," Linda said. "The map's not wrong. It can't be."

"We'll find out soon enough," Tomi said as they approached the parked vehicles. He reached for the radio and spoke into the mic. "Sergeant O'Brian. Come in. Over."

"Sergeant O'Brian speaking. Over."

"I want you to spread out and keep an eye out for danger. Over."

"Got it, Sir. Over."

"Be careful. Over and out," Tomi added, though there was no real need. His entire team knew what to do. He replaced the radio and looked around the cab. "Look alive, people. Let's find out what's going on."

They cautiously approached the single vehicle and encountered a knot of people. It looked like they'd gone to hell and back, their expressions grim and their manner alert, but they weren't overtly threatening.

"Let me talk to them first," Tomi said, climbing out of the truck. He raised a hand in greeting and said, "I'm Lieutenant

Cummings from Vancouver, and Mayor Finley sent me to assist you on your mission."

A tall, dark-eyed man stepped forward, his expression closed. "Assist us with what?"

"The retrieval of all information and research material pertaining to this site," Tomi said.

"As you can see, there's nothing left," Seth said, waving a hand around. "And your assistance comes a little too late. Half of us are dead."

"I'm sorry for your loss," Tomi said, taken aback. His eyes swept the group, noting the various injuries. *Half? No wonder they're so grim-looking.*

"What exactly do you want, Lieutenant?" the man asked. "We are tired, hurt, and want nothing more than to go home."

"Alright. Let me lay it out for you. I'm confiscating this vehicle and everything in it except your personal belongings. You may keep your weapons in case we are attacked, but I want no trouble from you."

"What else?" the man asked.

"We'll escort you to Vancouver, and you are free to do as you please from there. You are not in any trouble or under arrest. Except for a woman named Lila. She will be handed over into my custody along with her personal belongings."

"That will be a problem," the man said. "Lila is dead along with her accomplice, Daniel. You're welcome to their stuff, but their bodies are buried at our last camp."

"We will have to verify that," Tomi said.

"You can do as you damn well please," the man said with a shrug. "You have the big guns, after all."

Tomi smothered a smile. There was something about the dark-eyed man with the scar on his face that he liked. He's got guts.

A woman stepped forward, holding out two bags. "This belonged to Daniel and Lila."

"Thank you for your cooperation," Tomi said.

"So, what do you want us to do?" the man asked.

"Do? Nothing. You can rest while we search the site, catalog your supplies, and verify your story. After that, you can rest easy knowing you'll have an armed escort to take you home."

"And you promise nothing will happen to us?" the man pressed.

"As far as it is in my ability to do so, I swear on my life," Tomi said.

"Then I believe we have a deal, Lieutenant," the man said, sticking out his hand.

"Who am I dealing with?" Tomi asked.

"Seth. My name is Seth Waddell, and these are my friends."

They shook on it, and the deal was struck.

Chapter 21

The convoy rumbled across the broken track with Lieutenant Cummings' Humvee in the lead. Rogue, Seth, Jessica, Bear, and Imogen drove together, squeezed into the cab like sardines. Tomi's team drove the other three vehicles belonging to Ronan. They now belonged to any surviving family members and would be distributed according to Ronan's will.

The second Humvee brought up the rear for safety reasons, and Rogue had to admit she felt better knowing two giant-ass guns were looking out for them.

"What do you think will happen in Vancouver?" she asked, turning to Seth. "With the mayor, I mean."

"I don't know. We did what she asked us to do," Seth said. "We went to the facility, retrieved what we could—"

"Which was nothing," Rogue said.

"That's not our fault," Seth said.

"But we know her secret now. She had those scientists meddle with time, and we all know how that worked out for the human race before," Rogue said.

"Yes, it's not something she'll want anyone to know," Jessica said. "Especially not her detractors or the opposition party."

"We can use that as leverage to get the last batch of supplies she promised," Rogue mused.

"That's a good idea," Seth said. "And we'll be square afterward. We won't owe her or the city anything."

"We can start trade on an even footing with them," Rogue agreed, a smile blossoming from within. Then she noticed Imogen's wan expression. "I'm sorry, Imogen. I know we're talking about your mom here."

"I understand. My mother can be difficult," Imogen said.

"To be honest, I don't care about Vancouver or its mayor. I just want to go home," Seth said.

"Me too," Rogue admitted. "I'm tired, and I miss my family. Moran, Olivia, Bruce, and Patti. Even Ric."

"I miss my garden," Bear said, and they all burst out laughing. It felt good to laugh for a change, and Rogue felt lighter afterward. More carefree.

"Let's make a pact. As soon as we're done with Vancouver, we go home," Rogue said.

"It's a deal," Seth said, reaching out to squeeze her hand.

"I'm going with you," Jessica said, smiling at Bear. "My home is with Bear now, and I go where he goes."

"You're part of the family now," Rogue said.

"I'll miss you, though," Imogen said, her eyes tearing up. "I'll miss all of you."

"We'll miss you too, sweetie," Jessica said. "Maybe one day, you can visit us at Prime. Or we'll visit you."

"Maybe," Imogen said, wiping her eyes.

"Well, we're almost there," Seth said, pointing ahead.

Rogue craned her head and stared at the walls of Vancouver in the distance. "I guess this is it. Time to face the music."

Suddenly, the convoy slowed to a stop, and Seth had to pull over. "What's going on?"

"Good question," Rogue said.

She watched with growing curiosity as the lieutenant exited his car and walked toward them. When he reached the truck, he waved them outside. "Can I have a word, please?"

"Of course," Rogue said, exchanging looks with Seth. She got out, followed by the rest. Like a ragtag bunch of school kids, they waited for the lieutenant to speak.

"You're not going to Vancouver today," Lieutenant Cummings said.

"What? Why not?" Rogue asked, shocked by his words.

"Certain changes will take effect shortly after our arrival, and it would be better if you weren't there. You'd only get in the way."

"In the way?" Rogue cried, aghast.

"It's for the best," Tomi said.

"What does that even mean?" Rogue said. "For the best? Best of what?"

"We're supposed to report directly to the mayor," Seth said, stepping forward.

"I know that, but it would be better for all concerned if you simply returned home," Tomi said.

"I live in Vancouver. It is my home," Jessica pointed out.

"You can accompany us, of course. Imogen too," Tomi said. "But the rest of you should go home."

"You're not making any sense," Seth said, shaking his head. "What about the supplies the mayor promised us? What about Jessica and her things? Imogen?"

"And how are we supposed to get back?" Rogue said. "We can't walk."

"What's really going on?" Imogen said, pushing to the front. "What are you planning? It's got to do with my mom, right?"

Tomi sighed. "One question at a time, please."

"Just answer us, damn it. Stop beating around the bush," Jessica said.

"I can't," Lieutenant Cummings said, glancing at Imogen.

"Ah, this is about my mother," Imogen said with a triumphant cry. "You want her out, don't you?"

"It's not like that," Tomi began.

"Yes, it is. You saw what she did at the research facility, and you're going to use that to force her out of office. Am I right?"

"Not forced. More like nudged," Lieutenant Cummings protested.

"Don't patronize me. I've been part of the political scene ever since I was born," Imogen said. She fixed the lieutenant with a severe look. "Whatever you're planning, I can help."

"What?" he asked, his jaw dropping. "We're talking about your mother here."

"I know that," Imogen said. "I also know that she went too far this time. Dozens of scientists and researchers died because she wanted to play God. Again. After seeing what happened the last time people tampered with time."

"She's still your family. Your blood," Rogue said, turning to Imogen. "Are you sure about this?"

"My mother is many things: Brilliant, dynamic, and ambitious. She's also cold, selfish, narcissistic, and driven. Once she has her mind set on something, she'll never give up. If we don't stop her now, she'll try again."

Lieutenant Cummings studied Imogen through slitted lids. "What can you bring to the table?"

"I know all of her strengths and weaknesses. I also know who owes her a favor, who hates her guts, and who wants her gone. Most of all, I know her secrets."

"You know her secrets?"

Imogen nodded. "I can give the opposition a lot of ammunition."

"Fair enough," Tomi said.

"I only have one condition," Imogen said.

"What's that?"

"You treat her fairly. No public humiliation, no jail time, and she steps down with a full pension," Imogen said. "Maeve Finley has made many mistakes, but she's also dedicated her entire life to the growth and prosperity of Vancouver."

"Alright. It's a deal," Tomi said. "But are you sure about this? You'll help me depose your mother?"

"Yes, I'm sure. She's been the mayor for three terms, and while she's done a lot of good, the power is going to her head," Imogen said. "It's time for someone else to have a turn."

"Alright then," Tomi said, reaching out to shake her hand. "Welcome to the team."

"Not that I'm not happy for you, but what about our supplies?" Seth said. "We risked our lives for a final shipment to Prime city, and we can't go back empty-handed."

"You can take the second Humvee with the fifty caliber gun. It will keep you safe on your journey, and it's worth a lot. I'll even toss in some extra guns and ammunition," Lieutenant Cummings said.

"It's a start," Seth said.

"I will also try to convince the next Mayor to honor your deal and send a shipment of goods your way."

"Don't worry," Imogen said with a grin. "We've got your backs."

"At the very least, we could negotiate a favorable trade agreement for you," Tomi offered.

Seth glanced at Rogue. "A trade deal would be far more

beneficial than a single shipment, but we'd need an ambassador to represent us here."

"We could do it," Jessica said. "Bear and I can wait until the new Mayor is in power, negotiate a deal, and return to Prime with their offer."

"That's not a bad idea," Rogue said. "They can watch out for Imogen and make sure she's settled in as well."

"That gives me time to pack up my stuff," Jessica agreed.

"Then it's decided. You three will accompany me to Vancouver," Tomi said with a brisk tone.

"That's right, and together we'll make history," Jessica said. She glanced at Imogen. "In a good way, my sweet."

"I know," Imogen said. "My mother won't be happy, but it's for the best. Hopefully, she'll see that in time."

"Either way, I'll be there every step of the way," Jessica added.

Rogue blew out a deep breath and turned to Seth. "I guess it's just you and me, my love."

"I guess so," he replied.

"I'll make the arrangements for your departure," Lieutenant Cummings said. "It was an honor to know you."

"Er... same here," Rogue said, shaking his hand.

After shaking Seth's hand as well, he marched toward the back of the convoy.

Rogue looked at Jessica, Bear, and Imogen. "I'm gonna miss you guys."

"It's not for long. A few months, at most," Jessica said. "Pinkie swear."

Bear grunted. "We'll come home. Don't worry."

"Who knows? Maybe I'll come with them," Imogen said with a cheeky grin.

Rogue reached out and pulled the girl into a hug. "You're

always welcome."

She moved on to Jessica and Bear, hugging each in turn. Now that it was time to say goodbye, she didn't want to do it. "I hate this. Farewells are hard."

"It's not farewell," Jessica said. "More like a, see you later?"

"I like that," Rogue said, blinking back the tears. "See you later."

Moments later, Lieutenant Cummings returned and held out the keys to the Humvee. "She's loaded up, fully fueled, and ready to go."

"Thanks," Seth said, taking the keys. "Good luck with your err... takeover? Coupe?"

"Let's call it a venture," Tomi said with a twinkle in his eyes.

"A venture, it is," Seth said. He waved the keys at Rogue. "Ready to go, love?"

"I'm ready," Rogue said, though she wasn't ready all. Still, she had no choice. It was time to go home.

She gathered her things from the truck, said her final goodbyes, and climbed into the Humvee. Seth got in next to her and started the engine. The rest of the convoy pulled away and they followed until they reached a turn-off.

Seth idled in place while the rest peeled off toward Vancouver, heading straight for its imposing walls. "There they go."

"There they go indeed," Rogue said, her heart clenching in her chest. Already, she missed her friends. With a sigh, she looked away. "Take us home, my love."

"Yes, ma'am," he said and pulled away. Within minutes, Vancouver was nothing more than a distant memory.

The days passed without incident as they made their way back to Prime. It was almost as if the heavens made them invisible, or karma felt they were due a little luck, for nothing awful befell them. They never even had occasion to use the fifty caliber.

They traveled during the day, and slept inside their vehicle at night, wrapped in each others arms. Rogue's wounds healed, both those of the flesh and the mind.

Two weeks later, Humvee topped out on a rise, and Prime lay sprawled out before them. Rogue looked at Seth with stars in her eyes. "We made it. We're home."

Epilogue I - Kat

Kat wove through the crowd with one hand hovering protectively over her stomach. Not that she truly needed it. Callum loomed at her side like a giant, scowling at anyone who dared to come close.

She didn't mind. It was nice to know he was there, always caring and attentive. It made the long days pass quickly. Days spent in enforced inactivity while she waited for the babe to be born. She was on strict orders from Dr. Bloomberg not to over-exert herself. A tedious sentence in her eyes.

But today was different. Today the entire city celebrated the wedding of Patti Fry and Lee Alexander, a likable couple with no enemies. It was the kind of celebration guaranteed to bring the whole town out in joyous festivity, and she'd ensured that it looked the part.

Banners, balloons, flowers, streamers, and more decorated the city square. Market stalls sold delicious treats meant to tempt the senses, and a music band played on the center stage. Girls ran around handing out flower garlands and roses from the hotel's gardens, and boys offered tokens to free pony and camel rides.

"Ye did well, lass," Callum said with an approving nod. "Tis even better than I expected."

"Did you ever doubt me?" she asked with a raised eyebrow.

"Never, my sweet. How could I when ye're such an accomplished woman," he said with a wink.

"I'm glad you realize how lucky you are," she said, leaning into his side.

"Lucky indeed."

"Come on. We have to hurry. The ceremony will start soon," Kat said.

They sat down in their seats, those reserved for close family and friends. They didn't have to wait long. The entire city of Prime was out in force, and Patti did not keep them hanging.

A small instrumental band played the wedding march, and Lee took his place next to the priest. He looked every bit the part of the nervous bridegroom, tugging at his collar as if it were trying to strangle him. A couple of flower girls skipped past, throwing petals in the air, followed by a trio of bridesmaids in sunshine yellow.

Finally, Patti appeared looking regal in a dress made from pale yellow silk. The color complimented her auburn hair, and her green eyes sparkled. She walked down the aisle with the citizens cheering her on. Young and old, it didn't matter. They were all there to witness the ceremony.

They exchanged vows, followed by the rings, and all of Prime held its collective breath as the priest announced the moment they'd all been waiting for: I now declare you husband and wife.

A wild cheer rang around the square, drowning out the band and the church bells. People broke into song and dance, and Kat struggled to hold back the tears.

"Are ye crying, lass?" Callum asked with a hint of amusement.

"Yes, I am, and so what? Doesn't she look beautiful?"

"That she does, lass, and it's an auspicious occasion for us all," he said.

"Yes, it is. Look how happy the people are," Kat said, waving a hand at the masses.

"They'll be even happier when the free booze arrives," Callum said with a snort.

"Don't be such a cynic. It was a lovely ceremony," Kat said, slapping him on the shoulder.

Callum laughed. "I'm just teasing ye, lass."

Kat grinned, and she reached out to clasp his hand. "Care to dance?"

"Can ye? Being the size of a whale and all?"

Kat gasped, pretending to be outraged. "I'll outdance the lot of you."

"Alright, but remember what the doctor said," Callum admonished.

"Oh, come on. It's only one dance," Kat pleaded.

Callum gave in. "For you, lass, I'd do anything. Anything in the world."

Secure in the warmth of his love, Kat gave in to the moment. As Callum swung her around the dance floor, she tossed her head back and imagined she could fly, and in a way, she could. All because of him.

Epilogue II - Sandi

The cart rattled over the rough track, a single horse drawing it toward their destination: The Zoo. Sandi sat in the seat next to Paul, a rifle held across her knees. A blanket around her legs kept her warm, and her body was encased in layers of wool and cotton.

The cart in front of them carried Olivia and Jamie and three more wagons loaded with building supplies brought up the rear. Armed guards circled the convoy while scouts ranged ahead, looking for danger.

"How much further is it?" Sandi asked.

"We're almost there," Paul said, flashing her a smile.

Sandi sighed with relief. She didn't feel like her usual self and regretted coming on this journey. Her back ached horribly, and her ass had gone numb from sitting on the hard seat. Yawning, she leaned against Paul's shoulder and closed her eyes. *Why am I so tired all of the time? It's not like me.*

Paul noticed the state she was in and said, "Go ahead. I'll wake you when we get there."

"Thanks," she said and dozed off within seconds.

What felt like hours later, a hand shook her shoulder. "Wake up, sweetie. We're here."

"Huh?" Sandi mumbled, blinking into the light.

161

"We're here," Paul repeated.

Sandi sat up straight and rubbed her eyes. Then she looked around and gasped. The world that met her gaze was both achingly familiar and utterly alien at the same time. "It looks the same, and yet, it doesn't."

"I know what you mean," Paul said.

The clearing was identical to the one from her memories: A wide-open field of knee-high grass hemmed in on all sides by the primordial forest. A rocky outcrop ran along one side, topped by a guard tower, abandoned and derelict.

The ground sloped upward as they neared the middle, granting a clear view all around. There sat the remains of the old Portland Zoo, a place that became a refuge to the survivors of the Shift more than two decades before.

It was also Sandi's home, or it used to be until General Sikes burned it to the ground. Now, little remained but scorched beams, blackened walls, and overgrown roads. Even the wells were useless. The pumps were broken, and the water was full of mud and algae. It did not resemble the place she remembered. Instead, it looked strange and unfamiliar.

"It's so sad," Sandi whispered, clinging to Paul. "We used to love it here, and now it's all gone."

"I know," Paul said, his tone bleak.

Together, they climbed down from the cart and walked closer to the ruins. Olivia and Jamie joined them, and they stood shoulder-to-shoulder on the border of their old domain. A broken kingdom.

But there was still hope.

Ric wasted no time and got to work the moment they arrived. He barked out orders left and right, assigning guards to the old towers for security. With scouts ranging the area, a handful of workers set up camp while others revived sections of the old wall and repaired the broken defenses. Mules and camels dragged burnt stumps aside and pulled over damaged houses while dredges cleared the wells.

Dozens of tents cropped up like mushrooms on a rotten log. They circled a central clearing equipped with a bonfire and supply wagon. The resident cook began preparations for dinner, and the handlers built a corral for the animals. Within minutes, the area teemed with new life and the promise of a better future.

"It's amazing," Sandi said, gazing at the scene with wonder.

"That it is," Paul agreed.

"It's like I'm watching a miracle unfold," Jamie said with a hitch in her throat. "I wish Brittany was here to see this."

"I'm sure she is," Sandi assured Jamie. "She lives on in all of us."

"I know, but I still miss her," Jamie said, wiping a tear from her cheek. "Every day."

"We all do," Sandi said, a knot forming in her throat. "If I close my eyes, I can almost see us kids running amok in the Zoo. It was such a magical place for a child to grow up in. Full of exiting creatures, strange beasts, and whimsical adventures."

"Well, here we are, standing on the brink of a new dawn," Jamie said. "Hopefully, your children will be lucky enough to have the same experiences you did."

"That would be wonderful," Sandi said, flashing a look at Paul.

"Is that what you want, sweetheart? To stay here?" he asked.

"I think so, but what about you?" she asked.

"I feel the same. Things have changed, and I feel we're ready to take on our responsibilities now."

"What about the Watch? Bruce and Callum?"

"They don't need me. The Zoo does," Paul said.

"I feel bad for dropping Kat," Sandi admitted. "But, you're right. The Zoo needs us more than they do. Our future is here."

He reached out to squeeze her hand. "Together, we can make it work."

"Yes, we can."

"So, you're staying?" Jamie asked.

Sandi nodded. "We're staying."

"Oh, Ric will be so pleased to have you both on the council. Young blood. That's exactly what we need," Jamie cried. "I'll tell him the happy news." Before anyone could say a word, she rushed off in search of Ric.

"Well, that's that," Sandi said with a wry smile. "There's no going back now!"

"It seems not," Paul said with a low laugh.

"You're making the right decision, I'm sure of it," Olivia said. "Especially now that you're pregnant."

"Pregnant? I'm pregnant?" Sandi cried.

"Oh, my. I'm so sorry," Olivia cried, clapping a hand over her mouth. "I thought you knew!"

"You're pregnant?" Paul yelled.

"How should I know?" Sandi yelled back.

"How don't you know?" Paul asked.

"I'm a woman, not a psychic," Sandi said. "I thought I was coming down with something. A bug, maybe." She looked down at her belly, still flat and taut underneath the thick jacket. "Can it be?"

"I knew it from the moment I first saw you," Olivia said. "You have that special glow about you."

"I can't believe it," Sandi said in an attempt to absorb the news. "I'm going to be a mom."

"Mom? That means I'm going to be a dad," Paul said with a look of wonder.

"It usually works that way," Olivia said in a wry tone of voice.

"It's amazing," Paul said, the shock clearing from his face. He grabbed Sandi and lifted her into the air, swinging her around and around until she squealed with delight.

"Okay, okay, that's enough," she cried. "Watch out, or I'll puke all over you."

Paul immediately set her down. "I'm sorry. I shouldn't have done that. What if I hurt the baby?"

Olivia laughed. "She's pregnant, not made of glass, Paul. The baby will be fine, and so will you."

"I still can't believe it," Sandi said, breathless with joy. She looked up at Paul. "Are you ready for this? Are you ready for a life as a husband, father, and a leader of this community?"

"I am," he said, smiling down at her. "Are you?"

"Yes, I think I'm finally ready." A sudden thought occurred to her, and she frowned. "But what if we fail? What if we let everyone down."

"Listen closely, my dear," Olivia said. "You're not perfect. Neither of you are perfect. You will make mistakes, and you will let people down. But as long as you try your best and it comes from the heart, you'll do just fine."

"Thank you, Olivia," Sandi said, leaning against Paul. "I'll remember that. We both will."

"It's my pleasure, dear. I'll always be here for you when you need me. Like I'll be there for Rogue when she comes home one day, and she will."

"Of course, she will," Sandi said, reaching out to take Olivia's hand. "So let's give her something spectacular to return to. A real home."

Olivia returned her smile. "Let's do that."

As one, they turned back to the scene of ordered chaos that was the old Zoo, soon to become the new and improved Zoo. A new home for them all.

Epilogue III

Rogue ran her hands through her hair. It was cut into a short bob with choppy ends, and the color shone deep red against her pale skin. A hairband kept stray strands out of her face. It matched her outfit, a soft lavender dress paired with leather sandals. The items were a gift from her mother, and she wore them with pride. After all, it was a special occasion, and she wanted to look her best.

With a spring in her step, Rogue left the room and entered the kitchen. It was abuzz with activity, and several smiling faces greeted her entrance: Olivia, Jamie, Sandi, Aret, Kat, and Patti Fry.

"Look who's up at last," Olivia said. "Did you sleep well, daughter?"

"Like the dead. Sorry I'm late, but the excitement made it hard to sleep last night. I drifted off somewhere around midnight and found it impossible to get up this morning," Rogue replied.

"I know what you mean," Sandi said, her golden-brown hair tied into a loose bun. It complemented her long, white dress gathered under the bust with a belt.

"You look lovely," Rogue said, flashing her a smile.

"Thank you," Sandi said. "Though it's hard to feel pretty

when you're the size of a T-rex."

Rogue laughed and grabbed an apron from a hook on the wall. "How can I help?"

"You can mix this salad for me," Sandi said, handing her a wooden spoon. "I'm afraid my back's about to give out, and my ankles are the size of balloons."

"I'm happy to help," Rogue said, taking the bowl.

She dug in while Sandi grabbed the nearest chair and sank into it with a groan of pleasure. "Ah, that feels so good." She rubbed her swollen belly with both hands. "Why won't this baby come already? It's been nine months, and I'm enormous."

"Don't ask me," Rogue said with a helpless shrug. "I know nothing about babies."

Sandi sighed. "Now, you sound like Paul."

"The baby will come when it wants to," Olivia said. "You just have to be patient."

"I don't know if I can wait much longer," Sandi said. "The baby's using my bladder as a kickball."

"I remember those days," Kat said, smoothing a hand over her flat stomach. "And I'm glad they're over. The heartburn alone was enough to kill me."

"Speaking of which, where is young Teagan?" Rogue asked.

"He's helping his father set up the table and chairs for the celebration," Kat said, "Though to be honest, I think he's more of a hindrance than a help."

Rogue laughed. "Now that's something I'd like to see!"

"You'll get your chance," Kat said. "They're right outside."

"He's quite a handsome young devil," Patti said. "He looks just like his mother."

"Oh, the little one with the dark curly hair and eyes that look like melted chocolate?" Aret asked.

"That's the one," Patti confirmed.

"I saw him with his dad earlier, and they couldn't be more different," Aret said. "They make quite a pair."

"That they do, and they're the bane of my existence," Kat said, and everyone laughed.

"How are we doing, ladies?" Jamie asked, inspecting the food.

"I'm done," Rogue said, finished with the salad.

"So am I," Kat said, putting the last touches on a plate of deviled eggs.

"Right, follow me with whatever you can carry," Jamie said, leading the way outside. "I'll send the boys for the rest."

They each grabbed what they could and made their way to the garden square. The scene was one of ordered chaos. Long tables decorated with wildflowers stood underneath the trees, and streamers of ivy, bowls of fruit, and bales of hay gave the place a festive air. Spring was in the air, and the chilly winter was no more than an unpleasant memory. The atmosphere hummed with excitement, and every face sported a smile.

Rogue put her salad down on the nearest table and looked around. There were so many familiar faces that her head swam, and she didn't know where to begin: Moran, Bruce, Jessica, and Bear were there, all the way from Prime and Vancouver along with Kat, Callum, Patti, and Lee. No one was missing except Imogen, and she had an excellent reason. Now that her mother was no longer in charge of Vancouver, the new mayor had asked Imogen to be his assistant, and she'd gladly accepted.

Even Goliath and Violet were there, grazing in a paddock not far away with their new foal, Moondrop, frolicking about in the grass. A horsey neigh carried to her ears on the wind, prompting a smile. It was a good day to be alive, and she had much to be thankful for.

Moments later, she spotted Seth and hurried to his side. He was talking to Paul and David, and the trio laughed like old friends.

"Hello, boys," she said with a cheerful wave.

"Hello, Rogue," Paul replied with a nod.

"You're looking mighty fine today," David remarked, eyeing her with appreciation.

"Thank you, David, but I'm here to put you to work. Jamie needs all hands on deck to bring out the food."

David groaned. "And here I was thinking you were my friend."

Rogue laughed. "You want to eat, don't you?"

David perked up at the mention of food. "I am hungry. Starving more like."

"Then hurry. There's no time to waste," Rogue prompted.

David and Paul scurried away, but Seth stayed behind. "I'm not leaving your side again. You look much too tempting in that dress."

Rogue blushed and smoothed her hands over her hips. "Why, what a flatterer you are, kind sir."

"Only with you, my lady," he whispered in her ear. "Now, let's find our seats, shall we?"

Rogue nodded. "Lead the way."

They sat down at the lower end of a table and waited for the rest to follow suit. One by one, the people drifted in and chose their seats until everyone was assembled. With the food on the table, all was in readiness, and it was time for the celebration to begin.

Ric stood up and cleared his throat. "Good morning, ladies and gentleman. To those who traveled from far and wide, all I can say is, thank you for being here to celebrate this momentous occasion with us. It's been many months since we began construction, and we still have a long way to go, but I'm pleased to welcome you to… drumroll… the official reopening of the Zoo!"

A round of cheers and applause sounded, and Rogue joined in without hesitation. It was an outstanding achievement for the Exiles and deserved to be marked with a joyous occasion. More than that, it was a chance for everyone to get together and connect in fellowship and friendship.

Ric tried to resume his speech, but it was impossible. Finally, he gave in with a good-natured laugh and shouted, "Dig in, everyone. There's lots of food to go around."

People handed out plates and bowls, passing them from one to another. The clinking of spoons and cutlery filled the air, accompanied by the quiet hum of conversation. Rogue filled her plate with all of her favorites, fielding conversation from every angle.

She looked around, and her heart grew full to bursting with joy. Everyone she loved was there. Olivia and Ric, still acting like newlyweds. Moran and Bruce, an imposing couple matched only by Jessica and Bear. Sandi and Paul, expecting their first child. Kat and Callum, raising their firstborn. David and Aret, following in their parents' footsteps on the council. Patti and Lee, the kindest people she'd ever met, and Jamie, the bravest.

It was a wonderful feeling to have everyone in one place simultaneously, even though it wouldn't last. Some would head back to Prime and others to Vancouver now that a trade route had been established, but it didn't bother her. It excited her to know that the world was a bigger place now—one filled with possibility.

As for the Zoo, while it was far from finished, the Exiles were once more where they belonged. They were home. *And so are we.*

The End.

*Turn the page for more apocalyptic adventures!

**Glossary included at the back.

Do you want more?

So we've reached the end of Primordial Earth - Book 9, and I really hope you enjoyed reading the book as much as I enjoyed writing it. If you did, please consider leaving a review, as that makes it so much easier for an author like me to reach more readers like yourself and keep writing.

This is the end of the series, but I have lots more to offer. You can check it all out on my Amazon Page: https://www.amazon.com/Baileigh-Higgins/e/B01LYMGFUG

Plus, there's lots more where that came from. Read further for a sneak peek at The Black Tide, a thrilling, post-apocalyptic tale that will have you on the edge of your seat.

The Black Tide - Outbreak
   Available here: https://www.amazon.com/dp/B078Y4TBRG

Prologue

The Black Tide. That's what they called it. Incurable. Unstoppable. Terrifying.

It began in China then spread throughout Asia and Eastern Europe, rolling across the continent like a tidal wave, killing everyone in its path. The death toll climbed, reaching hundreds of millions within weeks.

The rest of the world mobilized, but despite all efforts to stop it the Black Tide kept coming.

When the disease finally reached my home, the borders of South Africa, we thought we were prepared.

How wrong we were.

Chapter 1

I took the loaf out of the bread bin. It was moldy. Fuzzy patches of white had sprung up around the edges, intensifying to blue-green in places. I picked it off with my nails and popped three slices into the toaster. With any luck, it would taste all right, and nobody would notice. I wrapped up the rest and put it away. *Only two slices left.*

"Lexi, are you ready for school yet?" I called. Silence met my ears. "Lexi, we're gonna be late!"

"I'm coming; I'm coming." She flounced into the kitchen, dragging her school bag behind her like it was filled with cement.

Flopping down on a chair she stared at me, her expression baleful. My little sister was not a morning person. I made her a cup of tea with heaps of sugar, hoping to perk her up. At least, we still had a lot of that.

I gave her a quick once over and sighed. Her dark brown hair curled out in all directions, the ponytail sagging beneath the weight of the thick strands. "What the hell happened to your hair? Did rats try to eat it? What will your teachers think?"

"What does it matter? I'm like the only one there, Ava." She crossed her arms and pouted, bottom lip stuck out as far as it could go.

"That's not true. There are still lots of kids in school."

"Is not. Even Jenny's mom is letting her stay at home now."

"Who's Jenny?"

She looked at me with disdain. "Jenny's my BFF."

I snorted. BFF, indeed. *Kids.* "Well, you heard what Dad said, Lexi. You're going to school."

She stuck her tongue out before slumping forward onto her arms. I knew how she felt. I also hated school as a kid. Now I hated work. *Same thing, different day.*

The bread popped out of the toaster, and I grabbed the margarine tub. *Crap. It's empty.* I scraped the last bit out and stretched it over a slice. Putting it on a plate, I handed it to Lexi. "Eat up. We're leaving in five minutes."

She eyed the single slice of toast but didn't complain. "Where's yours?"

"I've got my own, don't worry." I picked up the second slice and waved it at her then crammed it into my mouth, swallowing the dry mush with a sip of tea.

"Do I get lunch today?" Her face was hopeful, and my heart clenched as I studied her pale face and dull eyes, the ordinarily creamy skin like curdled milk.

I tried hard to stretch our meager supplies and when possible gave her extra, but she was always hungry. We all were. It made me feel helpless. Reaching into the cupboard above me, I popped out three multivitamins and handed her one. It was one of the few perks my job provided.

"Sorry, sweet pea. Not today. But I'll see if I can buy more food after work, okay?" She nodded and ate the last of her toast, swallowing the pill with a grimace. I copied her, worry consuming my mind.

The shops were running dry. Food deliveries had slowed, and prices had soared to astronomical heights. Never rich to begin with, we now struggled to put food on the table.

My dad walked into the kitchen, "Morning, kids."

"I'm not a kid anymore," Lexi complained. "I'm ten years old." She held up both hands for emphasis.

He rolled his eyes and laughed, ruffling her messy hair.

I handed him the last slice of toast and a cup of tea with his vitamin. "Here's breakfast."

My dad took it with reluctance. "Have you and Lexi eaten yet?"

Oh, Dad. Always worried about us.

"Yes, we have. We're running low on supplies, though. I'll see if I can get more after work."

He nodded, fishing in his pockets. "Here. I got paid yesterday. Buy as much food as you can. It's the last."

He handed me the notes. It was a pitiful amount, the few hundred rands now meaningless in the face of the growing economic crisis.

"What do you mean last?" I took in his rumpled appearance for the first time. "Aren't you going to work today?"

"The mine's closed, Ava." He ran a trembling hand through his hair. The news had hit him hard. "They ran us off yesterday. Told us to get off the property. They even had the police there. People were screaming, fighting…"

"God, why didn't you say something earlier?"

He shrugged and looked away. "I'll look for another job."

My father would never find another one. We both knew that. Unemployment had skyrocketed. This was a massive blow for us, but I didn't want to rub it in any further. "It's okay, Dad. We'll be fine, you'll see. I've still got my job."

"Yes, but I worry about you, Ava. Working in the pharmacy is dangerous. What if someone who's got the sickness goes there? What if you get infected?" His eyes fixed on mine, concern showing in every tired line of his face.

Lexi followed the conversation without saying a word, her honey-brown eyes flicking back and forth between Dad and me like it was a tennis match.

"I won't, Dad. I'm careful. We all are." I pulled a set of gloves and a face mask out of my handbag and waved them at him. "Besides, I can't quit. We need the money. Now more than ever." To tell the truth, I was terrified I'd get infected. But we had to eat.

He nodded. "I know, but I still worry."

This I knew all too well. Ever since my mom died in a car accident two years ago, he clung to us with desperate intensity. My dreams of going to University quickly faded in the face of his need, and Lexi was so young; she needed me to look after her.

"It'll be okay, Dad. You'll see," Lexi piped in with the optimism of youth.

I looked at her and remembered what we had talked about earlier. "I'd be more worried about Lexi if I were you. She shouldn't still be going to school. It's too dangerous."

"I don't want her to stop going unless there's no choice, Ava. She needs the routine, a sense of normalcy. We all do. Besides, the Principal assured me they're taking precautions."

I wasn't so sure of that. What would a principal know? Hundreds of millions of people across the world were dead, with more dying each day as the disease progressed. Asia and most of Europe were in flames, America had closed its borders, while Africa was a bloodbath. The only thing that had saved our asses thus far was an airport strike over wages. It had prevented the Black Tide from spreading here before the WHO could issue a global alert.

Still, it had spread to our central cities, sneaking a ride in on the backs of refugees entering the country illegally. Hospitals and clinics had distributed antiretrovirals from stores initially meant for HIV positives. While it couldn't cure the disease, it did slow it down at first. Until the virus became resistant. Now it was speeding up. How much longer did we have before it showed up in our town? A week? Two weeks?

"But Dad," Lexi whined.

"I don't think…" I began.

"We'll see how it goes, for now, okay?" He held up a hand to forestall any further objections, and we reluctantly subsided. He could be very stubborn when he felt like it, a trait he had passed on to both of us in spades.

"Fine. If you say so," I replied, not bothering to hide my irritation. "Let's go, Lexi. Have you got your jacket? It's freezing outside."

"Got it," she replied.

She kissed Dad goodbye, but I walked out after giving him a nod, annoyance fueling my actions. Why did he have to be so stubborn? I ignored the twinge of guilt I felt at the defeated look on his face and stepped outside.

Our feet crunched over the grass, frost glittering in the early morning sun. I hurried to my car, a rust bucket as old as the hills. The doors creaked as we got in, and I suppressed a grin at the look on Lexi's face.

"Why does your car have to be so old? The other kids at school laugh at me."

"You can always walk. A second class drive is better than a

first-class walk."

Lexi rolled her eyes at that but refrained from saying anything. I loved these moments. Moments when we could act normally. Like the Black Tide had never happened and we were just two sisters, bickering and teasing each other.

I turned the key in the ignition. The old girl groaned loudly but refused to start. It took several more tries before she caught, and a cloud of white smoke billowed from the exhaust, much to Lexi's disgust.

The petrol tank was low, and I smothered a sigh of despair. Fuel cost a fortune, but I needed it to get to work. It was too dangerous to walk nowadays.

The cold cut like a knife, so I cranked up the heat. Our breath puffed out in little clouds of mist, and my fingers felt like ice, the knuckles raw and chapped. Winter was never my favorite time of year.

A look in the mirror confirmed that I looked as bad as I felt. The recent rationing had whittled down my heart-shaped face to a sharp point; the cheekbones were prominent and my skin as white as snow. Dark green eyes gazed back without their usual vigor, and I resolved to get more sleep that night. *Maybe even a decent meal.*

I glanced at my handbag with longing. Nestled inside was my last box of cigarettes which I rationed with ferocious intensity. It was unlikely I'd be able to afford more. A terrible habit, one that both Lexi and my dad hated, but I couldn't help myself. For now, I ignored the craving, turning my attention to the wheel.

On the way to school, I turned on the radio, flipping between stations hoping for good news. No such luck. The situation was getting worse, not better. "Fuel and food prices continue to rise in the face of this ongoing crisis. All South Africans are advised to stock up on essential items and stay indoors."

"Stock up on what? The shops are empty," I shouted at the radio then closed my mouth when I noticed Lexi's stricken face. "I didn't mean it like that, sweetie. I'll get something after work. Don't you worry about it."

She nodded but whether she believed me was a different matter.

"The virus spreads through physical contact. Wear a mask and gloves in public at all times. If you or a loved one exhibit symptoms, report to the nearest hospital or clinic for treatment."

I snorted. Treatment? What treatment? There was no treatment. Once you got it, you died.

"The disease first presents itself with typical flu-like symptoms. Fever, fatigue, coughing, sneezing, and headaches which progress to vomiting, diarrhea, bleeding from the gums, ears, nose…" The litany of horror continued, and I switched off the radio. It was depressing, and we'd heard it all a thousand times by now.

The scenery flashed by in a monotonous blur. Gray skies, gray streets, gray buildings. There were precious few signs of life. None of the usual hustle and bustle. People were too scared to leave their homes and barricaded themselves inside. Uncollected trash bags littered the sidewalks, a testament to the municipality's inability to deal with the situation. *And it hasn't even hit us full force yet.*

Lexi fiddled with her phone, a frown marring her forehead. Ordinarily, my dad would never allow her to take her phone to school, but I had insisted. If something happened, I wanted her to be able to call me. "What's wrong?"

"I don't know. It doesn't work." She shook it and tapped the screen a few times. "There's no signal."

"No signal? That's strange." I fished my phone out of my pocket and checked the screen. I swung it around in the air as if a few bars would magically appear. "Mm, maybe the network's down. It'll probably come back on again later."

The school gates loomed ahead, and I turned to Lexi. "Have you got your gloves, sweetie? And your mask?" She nodded. "Good. Now put them on and don't take them off, you hear me?"

She nodded again.

"I mean it, Lexi. Don't take them off, touch no one and if anyone looks sick, stay the hell away from them. Got it?" I said this every morning when I dropped her off even though I knew she was tired of hearing it.

"I got it; I got it," she groaned. "Why do I have to go in the first place? Everybody else gets to stay at home." That bottom lip stuck out again in a full-blown pout.

She was right. Most of the other kids had already been pulled from school by their parents, and half the teachers didn't show up either.

"I'll speak to dad again tonight, okay?" I pulled up in front of the gates and looked around. "Where is everybody?"

The road was deserted. Even considering the drastically reduced number of students who attended, there should still be people around. I looked at my watch and groaned. "Damn, we're late. Hurry up, Lexi. You need to go."

"Ava, look. The gates are closed."

And sure enough, they were. A lone piece of paper, stuck to the front, fluttered in the wind. "Lexi, stay here."

I got out of the car and crunched across the gravel. The

paper was a sign, scrawled and taped to the gates. It read: 'As per order of the provincial government, all schools are closed until further notice.'

When did that happen? Why didn't they call me? Or Dad? Or even announce it on the radio?

"Useless bloody government, wasting my petrol and my time," I muttered, kicking the gate. I walked back to the car still grumbling and slid in behind the wheel. "Wish granted. School's closed."

"Really?" Lexi's eyes widened with surprise. "So what now?"

"Well, I can't take you home. I'm already late. Guess you're coming to work with me."

"Yay!"

On the way, my mind kept looping around in endless circles. Something wasn't right. First, our phones didn't work, and now the schools were closed? I mean, I knew things were wrong, but this was sudden.

I never got to finish that train of thought, because I drove around a corner and almost plowed into a mob of people gathered in the road, shouting and screaming. They were carrying an assortment of signs and boards, their faces contorted in anger.

Chapter 2

I slammed on the brakes, and my car skidded to a halt less than a meter from the nearest protester. There were hundreds of them—the poor, the powerless, the desperate. They swarmed across the road while waving their placards in the air.

"Where are our leaders?"

"Our children are starving!"

"Batho Pele, People first!"

Most were singing and chanting, protesting against what they perceived to be the Government's failure to protect them.

Taken off guard and at a complete loss, I craned my neck while chewing on my bottom lip in indecision. *Do I go back? Push forward? Wait it out?*

Bodies jostled for position, flowing around the car. A scuffle broke out between two men, fists flying over an imagined insult. Glass shattered. A car alarm went off, the siren wailing into the morning air. I looked from side to side, taking it all in, then spotted a group of men climbing over the wall of a nearby house. *They're looting.*

The protest had descended into a riot. And we were right in the middle of it. The first signs of panic stirred within me. *What do I do?*

A loud bang made me jump, and Lexi cried out. I twisted around in my seat, and my stomach lurched at the sight of the enraged face screaming at us through the back window. The man slammed his hands on the boot and bared his teeth. I froze, unable to move as fear turned my body to stone.

Lexi gripped my arm, "What's happening?" Her cry shook me out of my stupor. *We need to get out of here now.*

"Hold on tight, Lexi," I answered, looking around for an escape route. The road ahead was filled with people, so I glanced back again into the eyes of our attacker. The only way out was through him. I hesitated, but Lexi's frightened face decided for me.

Gripping the lever, I shifted into reverse. As usual, it stuck. *Shit. Not now.* I pumped the clutch and tried again. Nothing.

"Fuck!" I screamed, slamming my hands on the steering wheel. Behind us the road had filled up, the mob circling like hyenas going in for the kill. We were trapped.

My heart pounded with fear. It ran through my veins like acid, burning away all rational thought. I looked around, but our window of opportunity had closed. I fumbled behind the seat with one hand, searching for the ratty, old blanket that lay there. "Lexi, get down. Now. Underneath the dash."

She obeyed without question, hunching up in the footwell, knees drawn up to her chest. I tossed the blanket over her, hoping the rioters would somehow miss her if they got in. Common sense told me they'd spot her straight away, but I had to do something. "Please, Lexi. Keep quiet, okay? No matter what."

She stared at me with a face as pale as bleached bone. She nodded, and I tucked the blanket in around her.

I pumped the clutch again, praying with all my might as I jammed the gears into reverse. Success! It slid in with just the barest hitch, and I rammed my foot down on the accelerator. The car lurched, bumping into a knot of people behind us before stalling.

"No, no, no!" I cried as the engine died. With trembling hands, I turned the key. It wouldn't start. I tried again and again, pumping the gas before realizing I'd flooded the carburetor. My last shred of hope died a miserable death. A chorus of shouts rose around us like hounds baying for blood. Bodies filled my view, jostling with each other for a spot.

"Ava? What's happening?" Lexi's tearful voice rose above the noise, and I placed a shaking hand on her head.

"Please, Lexi. Whatever you do, stay down and keep quiet," I begged.

A stone smashed the window next to my face, and I screamed, throwing my hands up. Someone pulled on the back door handle, rocking the car. Thankfully, it was locked. Another stone hit the window. It spider webbed, lines running across the length. I screamed again, burying my head in my arms. All coherent thought fled as I cowered, whimpering.

Then a different sound sparked a surge of wild hope. Sirens. My head jerked up, and I looked through the throng of people. The crowd shifted, rolling away from the car towards this new attraction. Through a gap, I spotted two police vans, the blue and yellow stripes a welcome sight. They stopped next to the road. An officer got out, his blue uniform flashing through the press of bodies. I sagged in relief. "The police are here!"

Lexi's head popped up, her face as hopeful as mine. "Really?"

"Yes, sweetie. We're going to be okay now." Lexi crawled up onto the passenger seat, and I pulled her into a tight hug as a rush of euphoria flooded my body.

"They're here to save us, right?"

To her child's mind, the police were knights in shining armor, come to save the damsels in distress. Right then, I felt pretty much the same. "Of course."

The officer spoke to the crowd over a loudspeaker, ordering them to disperse. Instead, they drew up in a half-circle around the vans and heckled him. He repeated his warnings, voice rising in pitch when they ignored him. I watched in morbid fascination as the mob refused to back down despite his repeated entreaties, undeterred by his uniform or badge. The mood turned ugly, and a prickle of foreboding ran down my spine.

A brick hurtled through the air, smashing into the officer's forehead with brutal force. He dropped like a stone and lay on the ground, twitching. The loudspeaker fell from his weak hands.

"Oh, my God," I gasped.

The crowd surged forward, swarming the vans. They ripped the hapless men out like the innards from a chicken. I caught sight of one cop, his eyes rolling with terror. He was young. Hardly more than a boy. A fist connected with his temple. He fell, curling into a protective ball. Kicks and blows rained down on him. The mob focused on him with manic intensity, pouring all their pent-up rage into the attack.

"Ava!" Lexi cried. "What are they doing?"

There was nothing I could say. No reassuring words I could offer. Instead, I pulled her face close to my chest, placing both hands over her ears to shut out the sights and sounds.

The beating continued until I felt sure the officer was dead. I could not imagine anyone surviving such an attack. When it was over, the mob pulled back, allowing me a glimpse. The boy didn't move, limbs splayed in a grotesque display. Blood spattered his uniform; his face was an unrecognizable mess.

One of the men laughed and prodded him with his foot. Another dragged over the unconscious officer from earlier, his left eye swollen to the size of a tennis ball where the brick had connected. A group of children, barely in their teens, laughed and pointed. One picked up a stone.

No.

I couldn't believe my eyes. My mind shied away from the senseless violence. It was something so far out of my scope of experience, I couldn't even begin to process it.

The child hurled the stone down onto the defenseless officers with merciless intent. More joined in, flocking to the spot like a murder of crows. Their taunting laughter rang in my ears. I squeezed my eyes shut, unwilling to look on. When I opened them again, the two men had become mangled corpses.

Splinters of bone shone through ruby red blood, mingling with the dust on the tar.

Tears ran down my face as I watched, still trying to shield Lexi from the worst. "Shh, sweetie. It's going to be okay," I whispered, not believing a word.

A struggle broke out as the two remaining officers fought back, desperation fueling their actions. One pulled his gun and fired a few shots. Most went wild, but one bullet hit a woman in the chest. She collapsed, a red flower blooming on her chest.

The mass of people reacted viciously, their cries blanketing the air like the buzz of a hornet's nest. I cringed as the hapless victims were stripped, pushed, punched, and jeered at. Unable to watch anymore, I shoved Lexi back down into the footwell and looked around for an escape route. We needed to get out of there fast before the mob turned their attention back to us.

Twisting around in my seat, I looked through the back window. The crowd behind us had thinned, most of the people being drawn to the spectacle playing out in front of me. I spotted a gap and gritted my teeth. "It's now or never."

I gripped the keys and turned. The engine chugged sluggishly before rolling over and catching with a roar. I let out a cry of relief. *Thank God!*

Letting go of the clutch, I reversed as fast as I dared, not caring anymore about the possibility of running someone over. People scattered, jumping out of the way with shocked yells. I clipped one woman on the hip. She disappeared from view, but I honestly didn't give a shit.

Faces and bodies swept past my window until we were in the open. I swerved to the right, prepared to drive off, but a final glance at the murderous mob and doomed officers proved my undoing. I froze, my foot hovering above the accelerator. Guilt churned in my stomach, alongside the fear and panic. I couldn't save them. I knew that. The knowledge hurt.

The two had been doused in liquid. Their eyes were wide, faces haunted. Their skin glistened with the sheen of oil, slick and wet. A man in a red shirt walked up, a grin on his face. He pulled something out of his pocket and held it up. The crowd cheered. A woman lifted her young child to her shoulder, enabling him to watch. Their faces, uniform in purpose, were barbaric. My eyes were glued to the scene, unable to look away. Red-shirt threw the object he held onto the men. Flames raced up their bodies, igniting along the path forged by the liquid.

Lexi's terrified cries penetrated the fog surrounding me. I jammed my foot down on the gas and sped away. Behind me, screams rang into the morning air. A pillar of black smoke rose up into the sky, filling my rear-view mirror. My mind was a blur, filled with voiceless cries of horror.

Minutes later, an entire squad of vehicles raced past, sirens blaring. They swept by in a blur of white, blue, and yellow. The Nyala anti-riot vehicles lumbered along behind their faster counterparts, a water cannon bringing up the rear.

All I could think was—You're too late. Far, far too late.

End of preview. Loved what you saw? Get the book right here:

https://www.amazon.com/dp/B078Y4TBRG

Your FREE EBook is waiting!

If you'd like to learn more about my books, upcoming projects, new releases, cover reveals, and promotions, simply join my mailing list. Plus, you'll get an exclusive ebook absolutely FREE just for subscribing!

Yes, please. Sign me up!
https://www.subscribepage.com/i0d7r8

About the Author

WEBSITE - https://www.amazon.com/dp/B09JPBWGQ7

Glossary

Primordial Earth (Book - 9) – Glossary

- Glossary terms are listed in alphabetical order and without reference to their locations within the book.
- Generally speaking, physical location references are not listed in the Glossary.
- Measurements are provided in both metric and US/Imperial units.

Achelousaurus - is a genus of centrosaurine ceratopsid dinosaur that lived during the Late Cretaceous Period. The generic name means "Achelous lizard", in reference to the Greek deity Achelous. It walked on all fours, had a short tail and a large head with a hooked beak. It had a bony neck-frill at the rear of the skull, which sported a pair of long spikes, which curved towards the outside. Estimated size 6 m (20 ft) long with a weight of 3 tons. (Wikipedia)

Alamosaurus – A genus of sauropod dinosaurs containing just one species that lived in the late Cretaceous period. (See Cretaceous.) Specimens suggest they could measure up to 30 meters (98 feet) in length and weigh as much as 79 metric tons (88 tons). For comparison, the largest living land animal in the present day is the African elephant, which can weigh up to 6.3

metric tons (7 tons). (Wikipedia.)

Albertosaurus – A genus of tyrannosaurid dinosaurs that lived in the late Cretaceous period. (See Cretaceous.) Specimens suggest they could measure up to 10 meters (33 feet) in length and weigh as much as 2.5 metric tons (2.8 tons). (Wikipedia.)

Ankylosaurus – A genus of armored dinosaurs that lived at the very end of the Cretaceous period. (See Cretaceous.) Specimens suggest they could measure up to 10.6 meters (35 feet) in length and weigh as much as 5.9 metric tons (6.5 tons). (Wikipedia.)

Ballistae – Plural form of the ballista, an ancient weapon that hurled large stones, javelins, or bolts. The weapon dates back to the 4th century BC in Greece. (Wikipedia.)

Bambiraptor – A carnivorous dinosaur that lived in the late Cretaceous period. (See Cretaceous.) The estimated size for an adult would measure 1.3 meters (4.3 feet) in length and weigh 5 kilograms (11 pounds). (Wikipedia.)

Brachylophosaurus – A genus of hadrosaur dinosaurs that lived in the late Cretaceous period. (See Cretaceous.) Estimates suggest that an adult could measure at least 9 to 11 meters (29 to 36 feet) in length and weigh as much as 7 metric tons (7.7 tons). (Wikipedia.)

Carnotaurus - was a lightly built, bipedal predator, measuring 7.5 to 9 m (24.6 to 29.5 ft) in length and weighing at least 1.35

metric tons (1.33 long tons; 1.49 short tons). As a theropod, *Carnotaurus* was highly specialized and distinctive. It had thick horns above the eyes, a feature unseen in all other carnivorous dinosaurs, and a very deep skull sitting on a muscular neck. (See Cretaceous.) (Wikipedia.)

Clidastes – A genus of large carnivorous marine lizards called mosasaurs. An average size specimen could measure 2 to 4 meters (6.5 to 13 feet). A large one could be 6 meters (19.6 feet). It existed in the late Cretaceous period. (See Cretaceous.) (Wikipedia.)

Corythosaurus - is a genus of hadrosaurid "duck-billed" dinosaur from the Upper Cretaceous Period, about 77–75.7 million years ago. It lived in what is now North America. Its name means "helmet lizard", derived from Greek and has an estimated length of 9 meters (30 ft).

Cretaceous – The Cretaceous period is defined as beginning 145 million years ago (mya) and lasting until approximately 66 mya. (Wikipedia.)

Dryptosaurus - Pronunciation: drip-toe-SORE-us, Name meaning: 'tearing lizard' Dryptosaurus is a genus of tyrannosauroid that lived approximately 67 million years ago during the latter part of the Cretaceous period in what is now New Jersey. Dryptosaurus was a large, bipedal, ground-dwelling carnivore that could grow up to 7.5 m long. Estimated Mass: 1 500 kg (See Cretaceous) (Wikipedia)

Gorgosaurus - *GOR-gə-SOR-əs*; meaning "dreadful lizard") is a genus of tyrannosaurid theropod dinosaur that lived in western North America during the Late Cretaceous Period (Campanian), between about 76.6 and 75.1 million years ago. (See Cretaceous) Like most known tyrannosaurids, *Gorgosaurus* was a bipedal predator weighing more than two metric tons as an adult; dozens of large, sharp teeth lined its jaws, while its two-fingered forelimbs were comparatively small. (See Cretaceous) (Wikipedia)

Kalama city - Kalama is a city in Cowlitz County, Washington, United States. It is part of the Longview, Washington Metropolitan Statistical Area. General J.W. Sprague of the Northern Pacific Railroad named the town in 1871 for the Indian word calama, meaning pretty maiden. It's situated on the mouth of the Kalama river which flows into the Columbia. (Wikipedia)

Lambeosaurus – A genus of hadrosaurid herbivore dinosaurs that lived in the late Cretaceous period. (See Cretaceous) These dinosaurs had duckbills and could feed on trees as high as 4 meters (13 feet). (Wikipedia.)

mya – an acronym for "million years ago," also "m.y.a," used in astronomy, geology, and paleontology. (Wikipedia)

Nyctosaurus – A genus of nyctosaurid pterodactyloid pterosaur that lived in the late Cretaceous period. An adult could have a wingspan of 2 meters (6.5 feet). Compared to terrestrial dinosaurs, Nyctosaurus were small-bodied and weighed less than 2 kilograms (4.4 pounds). (See Cretaceous.) (Wikipedia.)

Prime City - A settlement of survivors that formed around the former Prime hotel, owned and run by the self-proclaimed Senator Douglas. He used the Watch to patrol the walls and keep the people in line.

Parasaurolophus - Pronounced pa-ra-saw-ROL-off-us. A genus of ornithopod dinosaur from the Upper Cretaceous of what is now North America, about 76.5–73 million years ago. Its name means "near crested lizard." (See Cretaceous) **Length:** 11.0m **Weight:** 3500kg (Wikipedia)

Parksosaurus - A genus of hypsilophodont ornithopod dinosaur from the early Maastrichtian-age Upper Cretaceous. A small, bipedal, herbivorous dinosaur. (See Cretaceous) Length: 2,5 m (Estimated) Height: 100 cm Mass: 45 kg (Estimated) (Wikipedia)

Pteranodon (genus *Pteranodon*), flying reptile (pterosaur) found as fossils in North American deposits dating from about 90 million to 100 million years ago during the Late Cretaceous Period. (See Cretaceous) *Pteranodon* had a wingspan of 7 meters (23 feet) or more, and its toothless jaws were very long and pelican-like. (The Editors of Encyclopaedia Britannica)

Pterosaur – Pronounced "tero saur." Science considers pterosaurs to be flying lizards that are distinct from dinosaurs. There are many different species. Pterosaurs existed from the late Triassic to the end of the Cretaceous period. (See Triassic.) (See Cretaceous.) (Wikipedia.)

Shanghai Tunnels, Portland, Oregon - also known as

the **Old Portland Underground**, is a group of passages mainly underneath the Old Town Chinatown neighborhood. The tunnels connected the basements of many hotels and taverns to the waterfront of the Willamette River. There is documentation in the newspapers of the 19th century of tunnels and secret passages underground. Organized crime was the center of many of these stories. However, many of the more colorful stories claimed for the underground are controversial. Historians have stated that although the tunnels exist and the practice of shanghaiing was sometimes practiced in Portland, as elsewhere, there is no evidence that the tunnels were used for this.

Stegoceras - is a genus of pachycephalosaurid dinosaur that lived in what is now North America during the Late Cretaceous period, about 77.5 to 74 million years ago. (See Cretaceous) The first specimens from Alberta, Canada, were described in 1902, and the type species Stegoceras validum was based on these remains. (Wikipedia) Height: 1,2 m Length: 2 – 2,5 m Mass: 10 – 40 kg.

Spinosaurus, which was longer and heavier than *Tyrannosaurus*, is the largest known carnivorous dinosaur. It possessed a skull 1.75 meters (roughly 6 feet) long, a body length of 14–18 meters (46–59 feet), and an estimated mass of 12,000–20,000 kg (13–22 tons). Like other spinosaurids, *Spinosaurus* possessed a long, narrow skull resembling that of a crocodile and nostrils near the eyes instead of the end of the snout. Its teeth were straight and conical instead of curved and bladelike as in other theropods. (Brittanica)

Quetzalcoatlus – Pronounced "ket suhl kow at luhs." A genus of pterosaurs. Triassic – The Triassic period is defined as beginning approx 251 mya) and lasting until approximately 202 mya. (Wikipedia.)

Tarbosaurus meaning "alarming lizard") is a genus of tyrannosaurid dinosaur that flourished in Asia about 70 million years ago, at the end of the Late Cretaceous Period. Like most known tyrannosaurids, *Tarbosaurus* was a large bipedal predator, weighing up to 5 metric tons (5.5 short tons) and equipped with about sixty large teeth. (See Cretaceous) (Wikipedia)

Triceratops - a genus of herbivorous ceratopsid dinosaur that first appeared during the late Maastrichtian stage of the Late Cretaceous period, about 68 million years ago (mya). It is one of the most recognizable of all dinosaurs and the best-known ceratopsid. It was also one of the largest, up to 9 meters (29.5 feet) long and 12 tonnes (13.2 tons) in weight. (See Cretaceous) (Wikipedia.)

Troodon - Meaning - Troodon means "wounding tooth" and is pronounced - TROH-o-don. Length - 6.5-11.5 ft (2-3.5 m) long. Height - 3 ft (1 m) tall at the hips. Weight - 110 pounds (50 kg). Troodon may have been the smartest dinosaur, having the largest brain in proportion to its body weight (as smart as a modern bird). It was a fast-moving, light-weight predator that walked on two long legs. It had serrated teeth, long, slim jaws, and a stiff tail. (https://www.enchantedlearning.com/su bjects/dinosaurs/facts/Troodon/)

Tyrannosaurus rex – A bipedal carnivorous theropod dinosaur that lived in the late Cretaceous period. These dinosaurs could grow to lengths over 12.3 meters (40 feet) and up to 3.66 meters (12 feet) tall at the hips with a weight of 14 metric tons (15.4 tons). (See Cretaceous) (Wikipedia.)

Utahraptor (meaning Utah's predator) is a genus of large dromaeosaurid dinosaur that lived in North America during the Early Cretaceous period. It was a heavy-built, ground-dwelling, bipedal carnivore. Height: 1,8 – 2 m (At the hips), Length: 5 – 7 m, Mass: 300 – 1 000 kg (Adult, Estimated) (See Cretaceous) (Wikipedia.)

Watch – A security and/or law enforcement guard force as described for Prime City in this book.

Zuniceratops – Pronounced "Zooni ceratops." A genus of ceratopsian herbivore dinosaurs having two horns and a head frill. It is thought to have been a herd animal. Specimens suggest a length of 3 to 3.5 meters (10 to 11.5 feet) and a weight of 100 to 150 kilograms (220 to 330 pounds). Height at the hips was approximately 1 meter (3 feet). (See Cretaceous) (Wikipedia.)

The Zoo - A second settlement of survivors who'd made their home inside the old Portland Zoo. Because they were denied entry into Prime City directly after the Shift, they despise all Primes and call themselves the Exiles.

Special note: While every effort was made to use dinosaurs of the Late Cretaceous Period existing in North America, this remains a work of fiction. Certain creative license was taken in instances where it better served the plot, for example, the Utahraptor, Carnotaurus, and Tarbosaurus.